**It was a soul-shattering kiss.**

One that reached him in places he'd thought were unreachable. A gentle touching of the lips turning quickly into a light probing of their tongues. Hands grabbed hold, clinging. Breaths mingled as one. Dear God, it was the kiss that he'd feared so much, yet wanted so desperately.

Surprisingly, Zoey didn't press to end the kiss, as he'd expected she would. Rather, she reached up, winding her hands around his neck, and fit her body into the contours of his. And such a nice fit it was. So familiar, and yet so new.

"Daniel," she whispered, pulling back slightly. "We shouldn't be doing this."

Dear Reader,

My aunt met the love of her life when she was twenty. They had a whirlwind courtship and she married him within two months of their meeting. Sadly, he died before their first anniversary and her world turned upside down.

Her first vow was never to marry again. She'd had the love of her life and no one would ever compare. Her second was to move somewhere far away from the memories. She did move, and she never dated. Then one day she met a man on the train. He sat next to her…they talked. She refused him the first fifteen times he asked her out, but on the sixteenth she accepted, determined to show him such a bad time that he'd leave her alone. But guess what? She accepted his next invitation and many after that.

"I didn't want such a drastic change in my life," she told me. Change is what she finally gave in to, though, and she was rewarded with a blissful fifty-year marriage.

Change in your life's direction *is* difficult. In *The Nurse and the Single Dad* Daniel Caldwell is forced to deal with a change that moves him in a new direction. Both my aunt, in real life, and Daniel Caldwell, in my book, have discovered that making tough changes can result in something amazing. May all *your* changes bring *you* something amazing!

Wishing you health and happiness…

*Dianne*

Visit me on my website at dianne-drake.com or on Facebook at Facebook.com/DianneDrakeAuthor.

ISBN-13: 978-0-373-21513-3

The Nurse and the Single Dad

First North American Publication 2017

**Printed in U.S.A.**

# THE NURSE AND THE SINGLE DAD

DIANNE DRAKE

**HARLEQUIN® MEDICAL ROMANCE™**

**Books by Dianne Drake**

**Harlequin Medical Romance**

*Deep South Docs*

*A Home for the Hot-Shot Doc*
*A Doctor's Confession*

*P.S. You're a Daddy!*
*A Child to Heal Their Hearts*
*Tortured by Her Touch*
*Doctor, Mommy…Wife?*

Visit the Author Profile page
at Harlequin.com for more titles.

For my aunt, Lorraine White, who faced her
changes with courage.

# CHAPTER ONE

COFFEE. BLACK AND HOT and lots of it—his every-morning indulgence. It was one of the few things in life he could count on with any regularity. Something he looked forward to.

Daniel Caldwell took a sip of his coffee, sat the thick paper cup back on the round tabletop and then spread the latest edition of the local Seattle newspaper out in front of him. An article outlining the latest in fluctuating oil prices caught his attention so he settled into his straight-backed chair to read it. One article was about all he ever had time for, given that he only allowed himself half an hour of "me" time on his way to work every morning. The rest of his day was filled with hospital duties or the duties of being a single father to an active, growing three-year-old daughter who was always ready to grab his attention.

It was a busy life, a very hectic life sometimes, but this daily half hour at the coffee shop made him feel more human. He liked mixing and mingling with other people for that little while, even though he really didn't have the time, at this point in his life, to socialize. It was nice being around others who had no expectations of him. In his own personal scheme of things, that was a rarity.

Daniel took another sip of coffee and read that the oil experts expected a continued fluctuation in oil prices well into the foreseeable future. Not that it mattered much to him. He drove an economical little car that couple of miles to work every day and, like that grandmother-type driver who typically took the car out only to go to the grocery store, he didn't do much other driving. At least not during the week. On his days off, though, he tried to take Maddie to the park or down to the pier. She liked to throw bits of bread to the seagulls and watch the people fish off the docks.

Daniel glanced at his watch, regretting that his half hour was passing so quickly, but fifteen minutes of it were now over with. So he took another gulp of coffee and casually glanced at the shop's door as the bells mounted above it tinkled a merry welcome to the woman pushing the door open and entering.

She was attractive. More than attractive, she

was a beauty. Elegant and understated in a pair of navy-blue scrubs. Had he seen her at the hospital before?

Looking away as quickly as he'd glanced at the door, Daniel didn't want to get caught gawking as she made her way through the tiny tables for two and headed straight to the serving counter. But once her back was to him he looked at her again. Did he know her? She seemed familiar. Same curvy frame, same confident carriage. No, it couldn't be. On second thought, maybe... But her hair was lighter—a nice honey-blond now, which suited her fair complexion—and it wasn't pulled back into a tight little bun at the nape of her neck, but rather it was flowing freely to her shoulders, giving her an oddly feminine look. It was nice. Oh, and the glasses were missing. Zoey always wore oversized black-framed glasses that gobbled up most of the top half of her face. They weren't becoming on her, nor were they unbecoming. Rather, they'd been a matter-of-fact statement that she simply liked to conceal her beautiful face beneath plastic.

Zoey. One thing was for sure. He'd never expected to run into her. Never wanted to, actually. So should he approach her? Be polite and ask her how she was doing? Daniel thought about it for a moment as he watched her interact with the barista, a young man of about twenty who was sporting waist-length dreadlocks and a killer smile. He noticed that she tilted her head slightly to the right as she laughed at something the barista was saying. She was so upbeat. But then, Zoey had always been upbeat during her several weeks with Elizabeth, and that was one of the things he'd admired about her.

That, and her nursing skills. Exemplary nursing skills, in his opinion. Especially since she was doing a very tough job—one he personally wouldn't want to do himself. He remembered how she was always so optimistic about her work.

Daniel knew that Zoey's outlook had been a great comfort to Elizabeth during her final days, and for that he'd be eternally grateful. She'd made Elizabeth smile and laugh.

This woman at the serving counter now had the same melodic laugh he remembered. A laugh he'd come to count on during some very rough times. He could hear it ring out over the low drone of the background chattering in the shop, and it was still as infectious as ever. Made him smile just hearing it.

It caught Daniel off-guard when Zoey spun around to face him, coffee in hand. She turned back to the counter for a moment to tuck a tip into the jar sitting next to the cash register, then looked straight at Daniel—who glanced immediately back down at his newspaper, realizing that in the past several minutes he'd managed to read only one sentence.

He purposely kept his eyes down as she started walking in his direction, not sure how, or if he wanted, to greet her. Damn, she was a reminder of bad, bad times. Times he wanted to forget but couldn't, as they still haunted him a year later. Even so, as she brushed by his table, he forced himself to look up and smile. Her smile was returned through a pair of the most hauntingly *stunning* blue eyes he'd ever seen. Damn it to hell, he didn't know what to do now.

"Daniel?" she said, pausing briefly, her lips curling into a friendly smile.

"Zoey?" he returned. "Zoey Evans?"

She nodded. "It's been a long time, hasn't it?"

"A year." One long, lonely year since Elizabeth's death.

"So, how are you doing?" she asked.

"Pretty well. Working and taking care of Maddie… That's about all I have time for."

"I'll bet being a single father isn't easy. I'm assuming that you're still single?"

"Still single," he said, pointing to the chair

across from him as he rose to his feet. "Care to join me for a few minutes?" He glanced at his watch. "I have about seven before I have to head out to the hospital."

She frowned for a moment, then gradually nodded her head. "That's about all I have, too. I have a patient to see near here this morning, and I don't want to be late for my appointment."

He thought back to all the appointments she'd had with Elizabeth and she'd never been late. Not even by a minute or two. "You always were punctual," he said as he pulled the chair out for her then watched the graceful way she slid down into it.

"And you were always running behind."

"Not anymore. I've changed my evil ways."

Zoey smiled at him and sat her espresso down on the table. "Always being late bothered Elizabeth, you know. She said she could set the clock by your tardiness."

He hadn't talked about Elizabeth in so long... Not out loud, anyway. Although, she was always in his thoughts. But actually to talk about her to someone... The wound she left still cut deep and he was always afraid that it would open and bleed again. He'd gotten along without her this past year and it hadn't been easy, never easy, because he missed her so much that there were still remnants of a physical pain lingering. There hadn't been a day gone by that he didn't look at her picture, talk to her, reminisce...

But actually to talk aloud about her... Never. Not even to Abby, Elizabeth's mother. She watched Maddie while he was at work and there had arisen this unspoken rule between them that Elizabeth's name was not to be uttered out loud.

"I knew she hated being late, hated me being late. She used to fuss at me for it. I think it was one of the few things we ever really fought about. But I don't do that anymore, and I've got to tell you that being on time is difficult when you don't have someone behind you to push you into it."

Zoey took a sip of her espresso and looked over the top of her cup at him. "She was happy in her marriage. She talked about that a lot."

"So was I. Five years wasn't long enough." Future plans they'd made had been cut short by a voracious leukemia. It was the kind of thing no one ever planned for, let alone considered within the realm of possibilities. But Elizabeth had been diagnosed and three months later...

"They were five good years, though, and just think! You have Maddie. How is she, by the way?"

"She's resilient. Staying with Elizabeth's mom while I'm working. Being quite the handful most of the time. Lots of opinion. Lots of attitude."

"She's about three now, isn't she? The last time I saw her she was barely more than a baby, and I probably wouldn't even recognize her now. They do grow up fast, don't they?"

He gulped down the last of his coffee. "That's what I'm afraid of," he said as he folded his newspaper with the intention of taking it back to work with him. He did that every morning, although he never read it, and usually tossed it away as soon as he was in his office. "Grammy overindulges her, though, and I'm afraid that's contributing to some of her thinking. She throws tantrums and threatens to go live with her grandma if I don't do what she wants."

"Tantrums?" Zoey asked. "Why?"

Daniel grimaced. "It's difficult for her, going back and forth between her grandmother and me. She's so young, and her life is so…unsettled. I'm not sure she knows what to count on." He blew out a frustrated breath. "I mean, the poor child can't even count on seeing me every night because I can't count on getting home every night. It's like so much of life is up in the air and there's nothing I can do to change that. Not for either of us."

"Then be patient with her," Zoey said. "She sounds very confused, and I'm sorry to hear that because, from what I remember of Maddie, she was a very sweet child."

"I know she's confused. So I'm crossing my fingers and hoping she'll get through the tantrum stage without it leaving any permanent scars."

"We all express ourselves in different ways, Daniel. I expect that Maddie's expressing her confusion the only way she knows how. And I doubt that it will leave scars. Even at three, Maddie's on her own journey, and this is simply part of it."

"I know that, and I do understand what she's going through, but that doesn't make it any easier on me. And the way Abby spoils her..." He shook his head. "It gets in the way; I think Maddie believes that everyone should treat her the way her grandmother does."

Zoey smiled. "Aren't grandmothers supposed to spoil their grandchildren? I always thought that was a God-given right."

"But Abby goes to the extreme."

"Or you're just being overly sensitive to the only way she knows how to express her love. We all do it differently, you know."

"Maybe that's the case, because I know she means well. And she loves Maddie. In fact, when it gets right down to it, she's a wonderful grandmother. But Elizabeth and I talked for hours one night about our hopes and dreams for our daughter, and the way I would raise her once Elizabeth was gone, and it wasn't by spoiling her the way Abby does. Elizabeth desperately wanted Maddie to grow up strong and independent."

*"I know you'll take care of Maddie, but I want you to take care of yourself, too. Go on with your life, Daniel. Have fun. Be happy. Find someone to start over with. I don't want you to be alone."*

Yes, they'd made plans together, but Elizabeth's plan for him was so difficult.

"Well, I'm sure things will work out in your favor, given enough time. Oh, and maturity on Maddie's part. I'm confident she will eventually grow out of it."

Daniel sighed heavily. He knew Abby was trying to replace Elizabeth with Maddie, which was why he hadn't said anything to her, as Abby's loss was truly as great as his own. "I'd originally thought about putting Maddie in daycare at the hospital. But I'm a firm believer in family first, and I think Maddie can benefit from her grandmother, if her grandmother eases up a little."

"Then talk to her, Daniel. Be honest and don't hold back anything. That's the only fair thing to do for everybody involved. I mean, I met Abby a few times. She's a strong lady. Very opinionated. And she dearly loves her granddaughter, which is why I know she'll listen to you."

"I hope so, because I think it's good for both of them to be together, especially now, when the wounds are still so close to the surface."

"Like I said—have that talk. It will do you both some good."

"I will. And thanks for the advice. I haven't had anyone to talk to in a while and this has been...pleasant." He smiled, and pushed back from the table. "Look, I've got to go. I have three residents and five med students waiting to do rounds with me this morning, then I've got a meeting at nine and at least a dozen patients to see, not to mention reading charts, revising orders, et cetera, et cetera..."

"I take it you're still a hospitalist?"

"Still and always. Private practice isn't my thing. It's too confining. I like the variety you get working general duty in a hospital. It keeps you on your toes, and you never get bored."

"Then private practice bores you?"

"Can't say one way or another, since I've never been in one. But I can't imagine myself contained for very long in one office. The case work may vary patient by patient but I think that overall it would be too restrictive for me. No, I like the open spaces of the hospital, where I'm free to wander at will."

"At will?"

"OK. Maybe not at will so much as what the caseload dictates." He chuckled. "And it dictates pretty loudly sometimes. So, do you get over to the hospital very often?"

"Not really. Even though I work for the hospital, I'm based out of an office across the street, and I only go over there maybe twice a week. And then it's in and out as quickly as I can. Hospitals aren't my strong suit."

"Why not?"

"Well, you like the big, open spaces of them, while I prefer to practice my nursing in a more intimate setting."

"Which is why you're in home care."

"I *love* home care. Home is where my patients are the happiest."

"But hospice nursing? That's tough."

"And rewarding. I started doing it when I was working on my graduate degree because the hours worked with my school schedule, discovered I loved it, and I've never found a reason to change to any other kind of nursing specialty."

"Like I say, tough work. Losing a patient is never easy but to lose every single one of them?"

She shrugged. "What can I say? I like giving support and care at the end. It's important work and most people aren't cut out to do it. I happen to be one of those who is."

"So, we're both happy where we are."

"That's a good thing, isn't it?"

He nodded. "We ought to do coffee again sometime. It was…nice."

"I would, but I don't wander into this neighborhood at this time of day unless the circumstances call for it. Mrs. Barrow, the lady I'll be seeing this morning, is an everyday after-lunch call, but I had to move her up today due to a doctor's appointment this afternoon. And this little coffee shop was right on the way to her house. Except for today, I usually stop here around noon or one."

"So we miss each other by roughly six hours on a normal day."

"Apparently we do."

"Well, maybe I'll pop in at noon sometime."

"And maybe I'll be here."

Daniel stepped away from the table. "I've

really got to be going now, so thanks for the company. It was nice bumping into you again."

"Thank *you*."

They parted company and Daniel didn't look back at the beauty who remained sitting at the table sipping her espresso. At least, not until he was outside. Then he looked back in through the plate-glass window and watched her for a moment. In all the weeks she'd come to his house to care for Elizabeth, he couldn't remember ever having had a real conversation with her about anything other than Elizabeth.

Turned out Zoey Evans was nice to chat with. And so easy. He was surprised by the ease he'd felt in talking to her. In fact, he wouldn't mind bumping into her again. It would have to be another coincidence, though, as he wasn't at a place in his life where he could go out of the way to expand his relationship horizons. Right now, everything was too complicated. But the prospect of seeing Zoey again, well, that almost excited him. It made him feel guilty, too, because it felt like his excitement to see Zoey was betraying Elizabeth. And he didn't want to feel that way when he was trying hard to push himself forward in his life.

Daniel Caldwell. It had been a year since she'd last seen him and what a difference that year had made. He'd been so gaunt back then, taking care of his wife and child, as well as maintaining his position at the hospital. Burning his candle at more ends than a candle had to burn. The stress of that time had certainly taken its toll on Daniel and, if it hadn't shown in the thinness of his face, it did show in the haunting, distant look she always saw in his eyes. It was a difficult time for him and she understood the toll it had taken. She'd seen it before in the families of other patients.

Yet, Daniel was different than most. He internalized his tragedy more than many people did. At least, the ones she'd come into contact with. And he'd always made sure that everyone around him was taken care of first, before his own needs were met. Even her. Zoey recalled how he'd always put on a fresh pot of coffee for her, something that had been totally unnecessary, but welcomed. She'd told him she could make her own coffee, but he wouldn't hear of that, insisting that every little effort helped the cause, which in Daniel's case had been his wife.

He'd been right about that, as the more Elizabeth had progressed into her illness the more help she'd needed, which meant the less time Zoey had had to attend to the little things.

Back then, she'd truly appreciated the kindness in a simple cup of coffee.

More than that, she'd appreciated Daniel's devotion to Elizabeth. A lot of people turned away in the last moments, trying to avoid the inevitable. Oh, they might be there in the flesh, but the rest of them would tune out. Not Daniel, though. He'd stayed right in there until the end, doing whatever he could do to help his wife, and also to help *her*.

Zoey admired that, wishing that she could have seen what appeared to her as the ideal marriage at a different point in time. It was hard for her to imagine someone being that happy in a relationship. She'd never been, and somewhere along the line she'd quit holding out the hope that it could ever happen for her. Her own failure at marriage had really knocked her off her game. Caused her to lack confidence in herself when it came to maintaining other relationships. Truth was, she wasn't sure she could do that again. At least, not with the same enthusiasm she'd had for her first marriage, tragedy that it was.

Zoey didn't exclude herself from the possibility of having something more in her future, though. Not entirely. She did have a little hope left, a dying ember. But she wondered if she could approach it with the passion she knew would be needed, as the passion had been dead in her for such a long time now. Brad had seen to that.

Maybe someday she'd settle down and try it again, since life alone wasn't that great. But not until she found all the pieces of herself that were still missing—the pieces Brad had stolen from her when their marriage had broken up. The basic hope that he'd robbed her of. The disillusionment he'd left in its place. He'd chipped away and chipped away until so much was gone. And she'd let it happen because she'd thought that was part of being in true love, naive as that might have seemed.

Yet, true love had failed her. And quickly. She'd recognized Brad for who he really was early on, and the rest of their few months together had turned into a futile effort of honing her coping skills, trying to figure out where she'd gone so wrong, falling for someone like him. How could she have been so stupid?

Admittedly, he'd hurt her. Not in her heart so much as in her confidence in herself to make wise relationship choices. He'd caused her to lose her bearings in all the things she'd always believed, always wanted. Even now, while she was sure of herself on the outside, everything inside her still quivered with doubts. The result of that was a lack of trust in herself to venture out again. She hadn't dated, hadn't wanted to. Hadn't even thought much about it. Turning her back on the whole muddy affair was easier and, until she was sure she wouldn't mess up again, she was perfectly happy right where she was.

Sighing, Zoey thought about what her future might hold. A real relationship? One that she trusted? Suddenly, Daniel flashed into her mind and she fantasized about how it would be nice to come home to someone like him. Someone who nurtured. Someone who was passionate about his love. It was such an illusion, though. Daniel was one in a million. She'd heard the affectionate way he'd spoken to his wife, seen the way he'd taken care of her. How he'd sat at her bedside for hours on end, simply holding her hand while she slept. How tenderly he'd kissed her when her pain had been so excruciating she'd been nearly out of her head. How lovingly he'd embraced her in her final moments.

Yes, she'd been granted such an inspiring look into an intimacy she'd never before seen the likes of, and that was when she knew that there weren't many men like Daniel out there. Elizabeth had been a very lucky woman to have him and, in a way, Zoey envied her for that because a man like Daniel was all she'd ever wanted for herself.

Would she ever find that man? Find someone who cared so deeply and passionately that nothing else in the world seemed to matter? Find someone to love her the way Daniel had loved Elizabeth?

Daniel... Zoey's mind wandered back to him once again as she drove to her first appointment. He looked good with those few extra pounds he'd put on. And his eyes weren't so haunted now. It meant he was moving on, and that was commendable, considering what he'd gone through. Some people got stuck at the mourning stage and couldn't get out. But he had his daughter to care for, and he also had his work at the hospital. Those were good for him. They gave him a great focus.

It had been nice bumping into Daniel today. As a rule she never kept up with the families of her patients once her term of service had ended. Some of them wanted to cling to her as a means of avoidance, but she'd found that a clean break was better for everyone concerned. So chance meetings like the one she'd had with Daniel were rare, and ever rarer was sitting down and talking to them. In fact, Daniel was her first, and she didn't know what had compelled her to sit down with him.

Maybe because, in theory, he was a colleague? They were, after all, employed by the same hospital even though they were totally isolated from one another. In the past year, when she'd had occasion to go the hospital, she'd glanced around, wondering if she'd see him. Their paths had never crossed, however, and it had never occurred to her to look him up. Because she *always* kept it professional, as there had to be divisions between personal and professional.

Not that she had a personal life going on right now. Go home, study case notes, feed Fluffy, her Persian diva cat, make a few phone calls, eat a late supper, do some reading and drift off to sleep. Repeat the next day. Then there were the weekends—errands galore. Grocery shopping, laundry, at least a half-day in the office putting charts onto the computer while no one was around to bother her. Plus all the other stuff she did on a daily basis. Oh, and wall-climbing on most Saturdays. She did enjoy that!

Occasionally, if she was bored, she'd treat herself to a movie with all the trimmings— diet soda and buttered popcorn. In the dark, no one cared that she was there all by herself, and it was nice to bask in that anonymity for a couple of hours. No expectations, no worries.

But every Sunday morning she made that obligatory call to her mother.

"How are you doing, dear?" her mother would say.

"I'm fine, Mom."

"Anything happening in your life yet?"

"Same ol', same ol'."

"No new boyfriend, no dating?"

"Just keeping to myself, Mom. And working."

"So when are you going to find yourself a nice man, settle down and give me some grandbabies?"

"Not in the near future, as far as I can tell. I don't meet eligible men in my line of work."

"So go work at the hospital where you can snatch up some handsome young doctor."

"I don't *want* to work in the hospital and I don't need a handsome young doctor in my life."

"You never change, Zoey," her mother would always accuse her. "You *never* change."

Same conversation every Sunday morning, and *that* was what never changed. But that phone call to dear old Mumsy was a habit she couldn't bring herself to break. So she endured it along with the rest of her obligatory chores. Then twice a year, she trekked home to Omaha for a week, to have that conversation in person. She'd gotten used to enduring the recurring topic in exchange for the week of pampering her mother lavished on her. That part was nice—being taken care of rather than being the caregiver.

As Zoey pulled her little red car into her patient's driveway, she looked up at the white frame house sitting atop a slight knoll and sighed. It would have been nice spending a little while longer with Daniel this morning. But duty called. For both of them. And her duty right now was to make sure Mrs. Barrow was up to a trip to her doctor this afternoon. Bathed, hair washed, dressed, vital signs stable, medicines administered... It was a privilege tending to someone who needed so much help, but Mrs. Barrow was one of the rare ones who was spunky in her end stages. Zoey liked that. Liked the feisty attitude as it made her feel a little feisty herself.

She sighed again as she headed to the front door, medical bag in hand. Something about Daniel had caused a restlessness in her. She didn't know why and wasn't keen to explore the reasons, but she wanted a date. Yes, a date. One night only. Wine and dine. No strings. It would break up her routine and prove to her that there was still a little human need left in her after all.

But with Daniel? She wasn't sure about that. He was a reminder, though, that something was missing.

# CHAPTER TWO

THE INSTRUCTIONS ON his invitation were perfectly clear. He was to be seated at table seventeen, the table all the way to the far right of the immense banquet hall, halfway from the front and halfway from the back. Two years ago, when he'd attended the hospital fundraiser with Elizabeth, they'd been seated near the front, directly in the center of everything, at a table with three other couples and a clear view of the podium. From prominent to insignificant, he thought, as he started looking for his table.

Daniel was never particularly keen to go to these kinds of affairs, especially ones that required a tuxedo. But Elizabeth had loved getting all dressed up and attending, so he'd been dragged along compliantly for her sake. He thought back to the lovely floor-length strapless blue satin gown she'd worn at their last hospital banquet together. It was stunning on her. His wife had been a head-turner, a real looker, with her long, flowing, sunny blond hair and inviting smile. Someone everyone had noticed, and envied. And he'd been the envy of every man there, having a woman like Elizabeth on his arm.

*"Go on without me, Daniel. Continue to do the things we loved to do together."*

Because she'd loved that night so much, and it had shone on her face, he'd been happy to be there with her. Proud, in fact. Then last year he hadn't attended as a single. It had been too difficult. Too many memories. And so much had happened in that year that the annual fundraiser had been the farthest thing from his mind when it rolled around again this year. Now, here he was, asked by his department head to be here.

"You're not getting out enough," Walter Downing had said. "I'm worried because, ever since Elizabeth, you seem to be retreating from the world. You need to shake up your life and get it going again."

Well, things in his life *were* shaking up, *were* gradually falling back into normal place. He supposed he should look at coming to this fundraiser as part of that.

Daniel did have to admit that this event was always a nice affair. The food was good, the entertainment was above par and the speeches urging those in attendance to do their part toward the benefit of the hospital were neither grueling nor long-winded, thank God! Tonight, though, he had an idea that he was to be seated at one of the notorious singles tables as he had not marked off the "plus one" option on his RSVP. Daniel Caldwell, alone. Damn, he didn't like the feel of that.

Sighing, Daniel made his way through the crowd and past the bar, where there were long lines of people waiting to be served. He bypassed the alcohol altogether, not that he would have minded a good, stiff drink to get him through the evening, and went off in search of his seat. The number 17 was clearly marked on a placard in the center of the table, right next to the centerpiece of pink and white carnations mingling with red teacup-rosebuds and snuggled into sprigs of greenery and baby's breath. Two of the chairs at the table for eight were tilted up, indicating that two people had already laid claim to their spots, then wandered off. Probably to the bar, he guessed. Interestingly enough, the two reserved spots were not next to each other, so the people who'd tipped up those chairs had purposely chosen spots on opposite sides of the table. No new friendships would be forged at this table tonight, Daniel thought to himself as he pulled out a chair and seated himself.

He glanced at his watch. There were still fifteen minutes to wait. A long, boring fifteen minutes, since he doubted he'd know anyone at the table, which meant conversation would be held to a bare minimum. At least on his part it would be, as he hated shouting over the noisy crowd in the room just to be heard. Well, so be it. That was fine with him, as he didn't have time for new friends in his life, anyway. These days, he barely had time to acknowledge his old friends, and on those occasions when he was thrown together with someone from his past it was usually someone he'd related to with Elizabeth.

Once, he'd lived in a world where his wife had been enough and now, without her, he was afraid he caused everyone around him to be uncomfortable. They didn't know what to say or how to act since her death. There'd been some invitations to dinner or other activities at first, more out of pity than the genuine desire to entertain him. But he'd always had the graciousness to decline as he didn't want to cause the ones asking him to feel ill at ease. Besides, he always had the excuse that he had to get home to Maddie.

Maddie might have been a convenient excuse on more than one occasion, but he truly enjoyed his limited hours with her. Wanted more of them. Envied the time his mother-in-law had with her, the parts of Maddie's life that he was missing out on.

"Is this seat taken?" The familiar voice from beside him startled Daniel out of his deep ponderings.

He looked up, then rose slowly to his feet. "You're assigned to the notorious singles table, too?" he asked Zoey as he pulled out the chair for her.

"Is that what this is?"

Daniel chuckled. "Always put off to the side where people don't have to observe our awkwardness at being here alone."

"What if being alone is a choice?" she asked, sliding into her chair.

"Then you'd prove the banquet planners wrong, since they set up all but one or two tables for couples."

"Ah, yes. The current mindset. Better off staying home than coming alone. But you're here alone, so how do you feel about that?"

"I'm here, but it's not by choice."

"You were forced?" She smiled and her blue eyes twinkled.

"Let's just say that it was strongly recommended that I attend this year. In other words,

I took the hint from my department head and came, although I'd rather be home in my jeans and T-shirt, drinking a beer, reading a story to Maddie."

"Well, I've never been to one of these affairs before, so I don't know how to respond to that." She picked up the glass of ice water in front of her and took a sip. "But I was pleased to receive an invitation. This was my first one and I felt honored that the planners would think to include me. Call me dumb or misguided, but I've been looking forward to tonight for weeks. Even bought a new dress for the occasion." She sat the glass of water down and looked over her shoulder at the crowd who were slowly migrating to their tables. "So do they expect us to whip out our checkbooks and make a contribution later on?"

"Well, they call it a fundraiser because there are a lot of dignitaries and corporate heads here, but the goal is to raise funds from *them*. Let them whip out their checkbooks and write the checks."

"Then why are *we* here?"

"To show that we all stand behind the cause."

"Which means they're showing us off as one big, happy family?"

"Something like that."

Zoey sat up straight in her seat and smiled at the man taking a seat across the table from her. "Nice size crowd," she said to Daniel. "Is it like this every year?"

Daniel sat up straighter too but he wasn't appraising the crowd. Instead, he was trying to catch glimpses of Zoey without her noticing. "Actually, it seems to get larger every year. I remember when they used to hold it in one of the hospital banquet rooms, but we've grown so much they moved it a couple years ago to this hotel."

"Hospital services are expanding, aren't they? I suppose that accounts for the size of the crowd—expansion equals more VIPs to court. Do you like working for such a large institution, Daniel?"

"Actually, I do. It offers a lot more medical services for its patients than a lot of other smaller hospitals can offer. So, since the goal of the hospital is to provide the best patient care we can, having better and bigger medical opportunities is a good thing. It allows me to accomplish more in the course of any given day."

"Elizabeth was proud of your accomplishments, you know. She mentioned that several times."

"Did she?" It was still not easy talking about

Elizabeth but, surprisingly, Zoey did relieve some of that anxiety for him as she was so easy about the whole subject.

Zoey nodded. "She said you made a difference. That your work here was important."

"Well, she was a little bit biased, I think." He looked around at all the tables beginning to fill up, frowned and shook his head. So many tables, so many people... Not really his thing. Although, the prospect of sitting next to Zoey all evening seemed good.

"You're frowning," she said. "Something wrong?"

"You know, I wish they would have put me in the last row. I actually asked for that assignment, but the organizers told me those tables are reserved for latecomers."

"The last row? Why? Because you wanted to sneak out?"

"The word *sneak* sounds so devious. I wouldn't have been devious about it. Instead, I would simply have said my goodbyes and walked out the door. Tux tails flapping in the breeze, I'd be in that much of a hurry."

"So your master plan was spoiled by your lack of proximity to the door?"

"Leaving from this spot's not so easy." He gestured to the back half of the room. "Too many witnesses."

"I could almost be offended."

"Why so?"

"You've got exceptional company at this table." The table was almost full now but the only two people sat down who were talking were Daniel and Zoey. "Including me. And I take it personally that you want to escape."

"Not *escape* so much as depart with an excuse."

"Excuse?" She laughed out loud. "Like you hate banquet food, or fundraisers, or large groups of people?"

"Is this a multiple-choice quiz? Can I choose all of the above?" Amazingly, he was enjoying this conversation. As he'd noted before, talking to Zoey was so easy. He'd avoided her all during Elizabeth's last weeks, probably because Zoey had been the constant reminder of things to come. That had been his loss, he was suddenly discovering.

"Just pretend you're at the coffee shop right now, sitting at your table alone, reading your newspaper. Maybe that'll get you through."

"Right. I'm at the coffee shop with five hundred of my closest friends, all of them wearing tuxedos and formal gowns." He cringed. "Think I'll get myself a new coffee shop. One that's a little more intimate and doesn't have quite the same dress code."

"Do you have a phobia about large crowds?"

Daniel shook his head. "Not really. It's more of an avoidance issue, I think. I'm not a particularly good socializer around a lot of people, and I get frustrated trying to put myself out there in a situation where everyone, frankly, doesn't care if you're there or not. I like small groups better, and one-on-one interactions."

"Well, I'll bet that a couple of double Scotches will have you dancing on the table before the evening's over."

"A couple of double Scotches will have me dancing *under* the table." The woman seated next to Zoey raised her eyebrows at the comment. "Speaking of which… Would you care for something from the bar?" Daniel stared directly into Zoey's eyes, purposely averting his eyes from the plunge in her neckline. It was a nice dress. Golden. Formal. Glittery. It looked good against his black tux, looked so much better than her everyday work clothes, which was the only thing he'd ever seen her wear. But her dress tonight was a little more revealing than he dared think about. Temptations like that weren't on his agenda. Not for the night. Not for the near future. And it was too soon to be admiring anything so tempting. "I'll be glad to go get you something. A glass of wine?

Maybe a mixed cocktail of some sort? Or a double Scotch?"

"I like wine, but not well enough to have you brave the bar mob. Or to risk you slipping out the side door when you have to walk by it." She looked over at the horde of people still mingling around the bar. "You did intend on coming back to the table, didn't you? Or were you going to use an errand of mercy as your excuse to leave?"

"I wouldn't leave you in the lurch. You're going to need that drink to brace yourself for the long evening ahead."

"See, you're spoiling this whole affair for me. I was looking forward to the evening, but you're bringing me down with your negative attitude." She tossed him a demure smile. "Elizabeth told me you hate black-tie affairs."

"'Hate' is putting it mildly. Want me to explain how much I hate them?"

Zoey laughed. "I think you've already done that. Which leaves me to ask you if you've got a diagnosed antisocial condition?"

"Nope. No formal diagnosis. But a lot of opinion on the subject." He smiled. "Starting with my parents and moving all the way forward to Elizabeth."

"And you've always been this way? You know, crowd-hater?"

"I don't hate crowds. I just avoid them when I can."

"OK, then. Let's try 'stand-offish'."

"It's not so much about being stand-offish as it is being a loner. I don't need a lot of people around me."

"See, I'm just the opposite. I love affairs such as this one, and big crowds, and being with a group of strangers who could turn into potential friends. I'm so isolated in my work that getting out is a nice change for me."

"You don't date?" As soon as the words were out of his mouth he frowned and shook his head. "Sorry. I shouldn't have asked. It's none of my business and it was too personal."

"It *was* personal. But I don't mind you asking, because my past isn't exactly a secret. No, I don't really date right now. Haven't found anyone who interests me enough to put myself out for him. And, overall, I'm not very trusting of men in general because I was married and divorced, once upon a time, and the whole situation left me nervous about trying it again."

"It was a bad marriage?"

"Almost from the start. Which, of course, I didn't see because I was too busy looking through the eyes of love rather than seeing what was really happening around me."

"Consequentially, you don't date?"

"Not that I wouldn't date someone, if he was the right one. But after I had the wrong one…" She shrugged. "It's left me more cautious than I probably should be."

"So how long were you married?"

"A grand total of nine months. Six of which were long and difficult." She took a sip of water. "He was a third-year resident who was badly in need of someone to finance his education and lifestyle. I'd just earned my doctorate in nursing so I suppose I looked like a likely candidate to him. We married fast, and divorced just as fast. And in the few months we were together he never stopped looking for his next conquest—someone with deeper pockets than mine were."

"But were you in love?"

"Totally. For about a minute. Then I finally saw the real man behind the facade and the rest, as they say, was history."

"Did it break your heart when it didn't work out?"

She frowned slightly. "More like, it broke my stride. Made me jittery to try again."

"Because you're afraid of getting hurt?"

"Because what I've discovered is that, when it comes to relationships, I don't have a clue.

I made a bad mistake once and I don't trust myself not to do it again."

"Aren't you being a little too hard on yourself?"

Zoey shook her head. "Better hard on myself right now than divorced another time later on."

Daniel looked up as a tall, gawky man in a red-and-black plaid tuxedo jacket took a seat in one of the two upturned chairs, finally filling up the table. "I'm Stan Kramer," he said, more to the air than to Daniel and Zoey. "I work in account receivables. I'm a section manager."

Daniel extended the courtesy of introducing himself and Zoey to Stan, then he fixed his eyes on Stan's gigantic Adam's apple as it bobbled up and down while he gulped his cocktail. After the initial introduction, Stan made no attempt to converse any further.

After the table finally filled up, the people there began to whisper amongst themselves and, for the most part, they turned into a pleasant, chatty group. Daniel did have to admit that it was nice to be around a bunch of people who weren't patients and who didn't want something from him. Although, mostly, he contented himself listening to the conversations of others, only participating when someone intentionally drew him in.

"You're not enjoying yourself," Zoey whispered in his ear. It was a statement, not a question.

"Actually, this isn't as bad as I thought it would be."

"But you're so quiet." She bent to the left as the waiter set a plate down in front of her—chicken *cordon bleu*, asparagus and balsamic tomato salad.

"Because I don't have anything to contribute."

"You don't really keep yourself *that* secluded, do you?"

He thought about her question for a moment, then shrugged. "I suppose I do. Elizabeth used to force me into the conversation—for my own good, she'd tell me. But, like I said, I've always been more of a loner." Unlike his twin, Damien, who was as outgoing as they came. Introvert and extrovert. Daniel had accepted his place as the introvert a long time ago. In fact, there were times in his life when he envied Damien his outgoing ways. Like now, when his twin was off on a medical adventure down in Costa Rica. Not that Daniel wanted something like that for himself, because he didn't. But he did admire the kind of free spirit that could simply take itself from one scenario to another at will.

"So, other than being threatened into coming, how did such a loner get himself here tonight?"

"By sheer will. It's an important event and, while I don't understand how my presence here makes much of a difference one way or another, I do know that the hospital needs all the support it can get. So I came."

"Kicking and screaming?" She laughed.

"Not so much. But I wouldn't be me if I didn't protest a little bit." He glanced down at the chicken *cordon bleu*; it actually looked good. Better than anything he fixed. His cooking nowadays consisted of whatever Maddie would eat, which didn't include a wide variety of anything. He'd mastered spaghetti and meatballs, or "sketti," as Maddie called it. His fridge was stocked with strawberry yogurt and there was always peanut butter. She'd eat a grilled-cheese sandwich, pizza and chicken nuggets, too. Most everything else was a struggle, so as often as not he found it easier to give in to his daughter's limited culinary preferences. A couple times a month, though, Abby would invite him to stay for dinner when he went to pick up Maddie, and those were the times when he got to break away from his cooking doldrums. It was nice to eat the occasional adult meal, and this meal in front of him now certainly qualified as an adult meal. After his first couple bites of the chicken, he sighed. It didn't disappoint.

"So I take it you don't get out much," she stated before she popped a forkful of the tomato salad into her mouth.

"With Maddie I do. On my days off. I don't want her growing up sheltered or…well…like me. You know…crowd-hater. As much as it works for me, I see how it can be limiting, and I don't want that for her. So I make it a point of taking her out somewhere every chance I get. Of course, I think she's in it for the pizza she always gets afterward."

"Maybe she's in it because she likes spending time with her daddy."

"That would be nice to think, but her daddy is a little stricter than Maddie likes."

"That's a daddy's job."

"Elizabeth was the soft one. Like her mother, she didn't have the heart to refuse Maddie anything. Which put me in the position of having to be the bad guy, the one who said no, the one who enforced the discipline that Elizabeth couldn't enforce."

"I can't imagine someone as young as Maddie needs much discipline."

Daniel chuckled. "I can tell you haven't been around kids very much. Three's precisely the age when a child needs discipline. It's a learning experience for them. Teach them young, and maybe you won't have to come down so hard on them when they're older."

"In other words, you're an ogre."

"That's a question you need to ask Maddie. She has a very distinct opinion on a whole list of subjects, and I happen to be at the top of her list."

"Then she's headstrong." Zoey scooped a pat of butter off the butter plate and spread it on a roll. "Taking after her daddy, of course."

"You think I'm headstrong?"

"I don't know you well enough to form an opinion, but my instincts tell me yes."

"I'll admit it. I'm headstrong…as headstrong as you are blunt."

"I'll take that as a compliment."

"You intend to be blunt?"

"I've *practiced* being blunt." Her eyes gleamed with laughter. "It's an acquired skill that I've worked on over time."

"Let me guess. You used to be shy and retiring."

"Something like that."

"Hard to imagine," he mumbled as he forked up a spear of asparagus.

He regarded her for a moment as she chewed a piece of her dinner roll. Bluntness became her. She wore it well because she wasn't rude about it. More like, she was practical or matter-of-fact. She made an observation and was honest when she called it out. He couldn't fault her for that. Couldn't fault anyone who didn't skirt around the truth.

"More like hard to overcome," she stated after she'd swallowed. "I was always reserved and quiet when I was young. Not so much an introvert like you, but always under my mother's thumb. She's pretty domineering and I was the recipient of that dominance. But, in her defense, I think she was that way because it was difficult for her to raise me alone and that was her way of making sure I was being taken care of."

"Do you still have a relationship with her?"

"A pretty good one, actually. She worries about me, but the way she expresses that worry is more like...well...nagging." Zoey laughed. "Sometimes it gets frustrating, but I'm used to it."

"And your father?"

"He split when I was a baby. Didn't want the responsibility of raising a kid, even though later on he got remarried and raised another family. And never had anything to do with me."

"Not even child support?"

"Not even child support, which my mother could have used, since she worked three jobs off and on to support us."

"So why'd he turn his back on you?"

"Who knows? Maybe guilt? Maybe he never wanted his second wife to know that he had a daughter from another marriage. I mean, I can worry myself to death over what caused him to do what he did, or I can think of all my mother did for me and be grateful she was strong enough to give me a good life."

"It was rough, though, wasn't it?"

"It was. But we got along. Anyway, Elizabeth said your parents live in Florida…?"

"In a condo on the beach. Living in grand style and loving the retired life."

"Do you see them often?"

"I haven't been down there for years, but they manage to visit Maddie and me about once every two or three months." He had a good relationship with them. Talked to them via the Internet every few days, mostly so Maddie could keep in touch with them and have a visual reminder of what they looked like. Emailed them occasionally, texted every once in a while when something interesting popped into his mind and snail-mailed pictures that Maddie would draw for them. All in all, he was closer to his parents now than he'd been years ago, when he'd still lived at home.

And it was a good thing, as Damien had practically dropped off the face of the earth in his newest venture. Sure, he snuck into civilization every now and again to hit up a computer for an Internet chat. He emailed whenever he could. Also, he called when he was near a cell tower. In fact, Damien even went so far as writing an occasional letter— short, to the point, often lacking in detail, but always welcome. Being in a remote jungle in Costa Rica might have hampered communication with his twin, but it didn't cut them off.

Daniel thought back to those very bleak days when Elizabeth had been deteriorating rapidly. He'd told his twin how he was feeling, how he was doing, how he was coping, and Damien had dropped everything to rush to his side to help him through it. It was such a relief to have him there—the closeness of twins couldn't be overexaggerated.

Sighing, as he thought back on those times, Daniel recalled how grateful he'd been to his brother for the support, and now he often caught himself wishing they could live closer together. Of course, Damien was happy in his life, where he was, doing what he was doing, and that was good. What made Damien happy made Daniel happy, as well.

Zoey was enjoying the antics of the comedian on stage who touted his credentials as a couple of late-night television appearances as well as his very own special on a comedy channel. A couple of his jokes had her laughing so hard she hurt.

"He's good," she said, nudging Daniel. She looked over at him to gauge whether or not he was enjoying the entertainment, but she found it difficult to tell as he had a polite, fixed smile on his face.

"He is," Daniel agreed, his facial expression remaining flat.

"But you're not laughing." She wondered what, if anything, ever struck his funny bone, or was he serious all the time?

"Laughing on the inside," he said.

"Which is no laugh at all." Elizabeth had talked to Zoey about her fears for Daniel, one being the way he drew in on himself. Was he doing that now? Feeling guilty for having fun without her?

"It's the best I can do. I've never cared that much for comedians."

Zoey sighed out loud and tried to refocus her attention to the act.

"What?" he prodded.

"Nothing," she said, biting back her response, as what Daniel did or didn't do was truly none of her business.

"I know what follows that kind of sigh. Elizabeth was the master of the provoked sigh, and I've had a fair share of them directed at me. So let me have it."

"It's not my place."

"It is if I invite you in."

"Don't invite me in. You might be sorry."

"Why? Because you're blunt?"

She tossed him a tight-lipped smile. "Something like that."

"I'm a big boy, Zoey. I can take it."

"But we're not really friends. Just passing acquaintances."

"We could remedy that."

"How?"

"Coffee later on. Something one-on-one."

That caught her off-guard. She didn't think he was asking her for a date, especially after what she'd told him about her dating life. Yet, whatever his intentions were, she was hesitant to be part of them. He scared her. Filled her with mixed feelings, as she could almost picture herself together with him. But there was always that one, huge drawback, wasn't there? First her father, then Brad... The men in her life had never worked out and she often wondered if her history was doomed to repeat itself. "Sounds nice, but I've got an early morning ahead of me, and it takes me quite a while to go to sleep. So, unfortunately, I think I'll have to pass."

"Suit yourself. But at least tell me what the sigh was about."

"Suit *yourself.*" She glanced up at the stage in time to see the comedian take his final bow and disappear from the stage. "You're here in body but nothing else, and I have a hunch you won't allow yourself to have any real fun. That guy was a riot and you never cracked your fake smile."

He paused before he spoke and frowned. "Elizabeth used to say the same thing about me—that I don't know how to have fun."

"You wouldn't know fun if it came up and bit you on the backside."

Before he had time to reply, one of the speakers appeared on stage and waved as the audience greeted him with thunderous applause. He was the CEO of the hospital, and Zoey assumed this was where he would make his pitch for donations. She looked over at Daniel and smiled. "Guess this cuts our conversation short," she said, leaning over so he could hear her. "But keep in mind that having fun is…fun. You should try it sometime."

He nodded in response and relaxed back into his chair, folding his hands on the table in front of him as if he was getting ready to take in every word of the upcoming speech. Zoey didn't buy that for a minute, though. Daniel had tuned out the room, the speakers, and probably even her, and he was transfixed in his own little world now. His eyes glowed a distant stare and she suddenly felt sorry for him.

He kept his life so compact that he didn't know how to open himself up to other possibilities. For another woman he might certainly be a worthy project, but for her, well, she wasn't getting involved any more than she already was. The last thing she needed in her life was any kind of a relationship that called upon her for a fix. And a relationship of any sort with Daniel would definitely require some fixing.

Not that she didn't have issues of her own. Because she did. But she had to solve those first before she brought anybody else into her circle.

Ten minutes into a speech that touted all the high points in the workings of a busy hospital, Zoey leaned over to Daniel and whispered in his ear, "So you think his speech will last much longer?" She wasn't exactly bored with it, but this was definitely not the high point of her evening.

Daniel laughed out loud and drew the scowling attention of the entire table. "I think he's probably winding down. But, if he's not, now would be a good time for you to send me to the bar to get you a drink," he replied. "Go with me and we can both slip out the side door."

"What, and miss the dancing afterward? You do dance, don't you?"

"Only under the table after a couple of double Scotches. Remember?"

So he did have a sense of humor! In spite of herself, she laughed aloud. "I'll take a glass of white wine."

"Large?" he asked, arching his eyebrows at her.

"Bring the whole bottle if you can."

"The offer of coffee still stands."

"So does my excuse for not going."

"Ah, there you go, being blunt again."

The older lady straight across from Daniel shushed him, causing Zoey to giggle. It wasn't the shushing so much as the incongruity of her appearance compared to Daniel's. He was decked out in a finely tailored tux while she wore a pink, non-formal floral dress with a large, flowery hat. She had champagne-colored hair and a sour squint to her eyes—a squint she was aiming straight at Daniel.

"Maybe bring her a drink, too," Zoey whispered. "She looks like she needs one."

Daniel pushed back from the table and arose to all his six-feet-plus glory. He was a good-looking man. Actually, downright handsome. Someone to swoon over. And the sour lady across from him nearly melted in her chair when Daniel turned a charming smile on her and nodded.

Damn, he had a way about him.

"I'll be back," he said, leaning down to whisper in Zoey's ear. "No escaping. Promise."

She'd never doubted that for a moment. Perhaps Daniel hadn't wanted to come tonight but he was, if nothing else, dutiful. She'd seen that in his devotion during some very rough times with Elizabeth, and she saw that now, as he endured something he hated.

Maybe she should have accepted his invitation to coffee.

"No!" she said aloud to herself. He might have some attributes she admired, but admiration from afar was all she was going to allow herself.

# CHAPTER THREE

DAMN! HE'D HOPED for a better result, but the lab tests only confirmed what he already suspected: Mr. Baumgartner had a long, rocky road ahead of him, with a questionable outcome at the end of it. His diagnosis: congestive heart failure—when the heart muscle quit pumping the blood adequately and fluid backed up in the lungs and chest cavity. Treated properly, it could be managed over an extended period of time. Left untreated, it was fatal. As for Mr. Baumgartner, it was too soon to tell what would happen to him. His case now was critical. Simply put, he'd waited too long for treatment and, as of this moment, he was dying. But Daniel hoped that could be reversed.

Daniel hated telling his patients bad news; it was the worst part about being a doctor. But bad news was everywhere, and it wasn't like he didn't have his fair share of cheery results, because he did. Every day. On that brighter note, however, Baumgartner was going home to adjust to the drastic changes he'd need to make in order to stay alive, and that was the best Daniel could hope for.

"Zoey," he said into his smart phone. "It's Daniel Caldwell."

"Daniel. How *are* you?"

She sounded excited to hear him. Almost animated. He counted back the days and realized they hadn't seen each other, nor had they talked, in nearly a month, but he'd thought about her. Oh, had he thought about her! Thought about calling her and hadn't been able to find a reason to click her number into his cell phone. Thought about dropping into the coffee shop some afternoon, but hadn't found a plausible excuse for wandering in at that particular time when she knew that wasn't part of his regular schedule. "I'm fine. Hope I'm not disturbing you."

"I'm with a patient right now, but that's OK. She's watching TV, and she'd rather not be disturbed when her shows are on. So I'm checking her meds, counting them to make sure she's taken what she was supposed to and calling in prescription refills. Which means, now's a good time."

Something was pulling at Daniel to turn this

into a social call, but the practical side of him dredged up the last time he'd asked her out to coffee. She'd refused. Turned him down colder than cold. Twice, actually, off one invitation. So he knew better than to veer off the professional path with her lest he returned with hat in hand. "Well, this won't take long. I need a professional favor."

"Name it," she said cheerfully.

"I have a patient, Horace Baumgartner, who needs to go into hospice care, and I'll be dismissing him from the hospital day after tomorrow. Is this something you can help me with?"

"Sure. Just give me the details so I can figure out what we need to do."

"Well, going home is what he wants, and I can't see any reason to deny him. He's still pretty active, though weak, and I don't think keeping him in an in-patient situation is advisable because I'm holding out some hope that we can reverse his course. I think the emotional boost he'll get from being at home will benefit him in the long run."

"What's his diagnosis?"

"Congestive heart failure, end stage. If he's diligent, we may get to keep him around for longer than what his condition dictates right now, but he's going to have to be willing to make some drastic changes to his life."

"Let me guess. He doesn't want to make changes."

"He's nice, but he's stubborn. What can I say?"

"Say that his unwillingness to cooperate is going to kill him. So, how bad is he?"

"Right now, bad. Blood chemistries are off, heart's only working at half its capacity, lungs are filling up with fluid, kidneys are sluggish, extremities are swollen."

"Well, it sounds like somebody's got his work cut out for him, trying to motivate the fellow. Anyway, call my office and schedule an appointment for Mr. Baumgartner to meet one of the hospice nurses. Talk to Sally, the office manager, and she'll get you started in the right direction. She coordinates all our hospice efforts, and makes the nursing and therapy assignments."

"I could do that, but I thought that maybe you…" Who was he kidding? He'd wanted an excuse—*any* excuse—to call her, to hear her voice. "You know… I thought I could cut corners by calling you directly."

"I can make the referral for you, but you'll still have to write the orders and send them over to the office."

He knew that, of course. But he also knew that he liked talking to Zoey on any pretense.

"I'll do that later today. Can I suggest you as Mr. Baumgartner's nurse, though? I've seen you work, and I know how good you are. And I want my patient to have the best."

"Are you trying to flatter me, Daniel?"

"Maybe a little. But what I said is true. You're the best, and that's why I want you on the case."

"Well, you can suggest me, and as long as the office approves, which I'm fairly certain they will, since I've only just had an opening come up in my schedule. So, go ahead and name a time to meet with him in the hospital, and I'll make the arrangements on this side of it."

"Any time you're free works for me."

"Shouldn't we be going by *your* schedule?" she asked him.

"My schedule is probably more flexible than yours, seeing how you have specific appointment times for your patients. It changes about fifty times a day depending on what's going on and I'm always at liberty to make those changes if necessary. So is later today good for you, or will tomorrow work better?" Was he going to ask her out to coffee again, or leave well enough alone? Actually, he didn't know. The practical side of him kept telling him to keep it strictly professional. But there

was this little voice—a nagging little voice—
that was taunting him to jump on in and try
again. Did he want to date, though? Or was
this more about making a connection to someone who'd touched Elizabeth's life in such a
personal way? A last desperate attempt to hold
on to something he'd lost?

*"Go on without me, Daniel. Go on... Go
on..."*

"Hang on a second while I check my schedule."

Things went quiet on the line and he strained
to hear anything in the background. A slight
hum pricked his ears. Was she humming a
song? He smiled, thinking about how nice it
would be to have that kind of noise in his personal background more often. Sometimes he
missed the noise—the little sounds that connected him to something bigger and better.

"I can see him at five thirty, make it my last
stop for the day, if that's OK for you. Also,
that'll give you time to square things away
with the office."

Daniel glanced at his watch. It was only ten
right now, which meant he had seven and a
half hours to wait. That was a lot of time in
which to anticipate something he wasn't sure
about. "That's fine. Come to my office first,
and we'll go see Mr. Baumgartner together.

I'm on the second floor; take the blue elevators and turn to your right when you get off them. I'm the fifth door on the left."

"Your name's on the door, right?"

"It is. And if I'm not in when you get there take a seat in the waiting area and I'll get to you as soon as possible, barring any emergencies." Emergencies happened all the time, but he'd be sorely disappointed if one encroached on his appointment with Zoey.

"Then I'll see you in a little while," she said brightly.

"A little while," he repeated absently, wondering if this was a smart move or not.

Zoey glanced at the time on her cell phone. Normally she didn't have time to schedule last-minute appointments, but for Daniel she'd made the exception. She'd thought about him this past month. Wondered how he was getting along. Wondered if he'd taken her turning down coffee personally. Wondered if he'd ever ask her again. In fact, she'd thought about him so much she'd even gone so far as to go to his office to see him. But when she'd gotten there she hadn't been able to bring herself to knock on his door. There'd been no reason for her to see him without making it seem like she was out for anything more than a casual meeting.

The thing was, she *never* went out of her way to call on families or friends of her patients. Daniel had turned into the exception, though. And maybe that was because he'd seemed so lost, and she'd let that get to her.

Zoey sighed, as she tucked her phone back into the pocket of her navy-blue scrub pants. It was a little after five now, and if she hurried she'd make that appointment on time. Warnings over what she was about to do were pelting her brain, nevertheless. Daniel was dangerous to her outlined plan for herself. She knew that as surely as she knew her own name, yet she couldn't define why, or how, that was happening to her. But he *was* dangerous, and that was enough to keep her aloof… she hoped.

With a fair amount of trepidation mixed with an equal amount of tingling excitement, Zoey climbed into her little car and headed away from her last patient's house. Traffic was unusually light for rush hour and before she knew it she was pulling into a parking spot in the hospital garage, purposely putting all her movements into slow gear.

*You can do this*, she told herself as she got out of the car and checked the rear-view mirror to make sure her hair wasn't mussed.

*It's not a social call*, she reminded herself.

Straightening up, she drew in a deep breath and braced herself for seeing him. "You're being silly," she whispered on her way into the hospital. "Silly!" The woman following her through the lane of parked cars cleared her throat, snapping Zoey back into the present. *Silly*, she repeated, only this time to herself. But, no matter how silly she felt, that didn't change the purpose of this meeting. Daniel had called her in for a consultation, not a date. To think anything else was a waste of time and good brain space. One professional to another; that was all this was.

Even so, she still felt daft, having all the telltale anticipation building up inside her the way it was. The question that kept plaguing her was: did she want to date a man who didn't seem to be over his first wife?

The answer was simple—it was a resounding no! She couldn't and wouldn't get involved, and thinking the unsettling thoughts was as far as she'd let it go.

The blue elevators she needed were just a hop, skip and a jump off the parking garage and before she knew it she was standing at Daniel's door, fist clenched and primed to knock. Two times in one month, she thought, cringing at the memory of how close she'd come to doing this last time.

"Zoey," he said, opening the door to her.

She blew out a nervous breath. "Daniel." Her heart was already fluttering and she was in a fight with herself to make it be still. What in the world was going on with her, anyway? It was a concern—a huge concern.

"Won't you come in?" Daniel stepped away from the door and gestured to a chair opposite his desk. It was a small office, not very impressive. Not particularly worthy of someone in Daniel's position, which surprised her. Maybe he didn't require much, though. Or maybe he didn't want the bother. Still, his office was tidy. Well-kept. No papers stacked on the desk. No books unshelved. Daniel was obviously making the best of very little, and she appreciated that understated trait in him.

"I'd prefer to talk as we go." The confined space in his office seemed much too intimate to her, as she didn't want to get *that* close to him. And behind a closed door? No, this closeness wasn't anything she'd planned for. "My office emailed the particulars of your patient, so I'm up to date on his medical needs, and I saw that other home-health services will be following him, as well. In particular, a nursing aid." She felt like she was babbling on about things Daniel had already set into motion, but she couldn't stop herself, and as they progressed toward the eighth floor she didn't quit. In fact, she was probably just regurgitating Daniel's own observations back to him. But, in her defense, she was nervous—not so much about the patient she was going to meet, but about being around Daniel. Even in the wide, open spaces of the hall.

"I'm glad you were able to schedule me in at the last minute," he said as he stepped back and allowed Zoey to pass into Mr. Baumgartner's room ahead of him. "I think Mr. Baumgartner will see that as progress in his favor. Which is something he needs right now."

"There's always a little leeway at the end of my day." Did that sound like she always hung around waiting for something to do once her workday was over? The truth was, there was always empty time at the end of her day, as she didn't have anything else to do, no place to go but home with her cat.

"Must be nice," he said, following her through the door. "Taking care of Maddie doesn't give me any leeway in my day. It's either all work or all daughter—mind you, I'm not complaining about either one, because keeping busy has been my salvation this past year. But I think I've forgotten what leisure time feels like."

"It doesn't hurt to take a little time for yourself every now and then," she conceded, trying not to imagine herself fitting into those empty margins in his life. That was a pipe dream, a wild fantasy that wouldn't work out. Zoey didn't like the direction her mind seemed to be taking her in, so she tried blanking out Daniel and refocusing on the frowning man in the bed across the room from her.

"Time to myself might not hurt," Daniel went on as they crossed the room together. "But I don't like the emptiness that comes with it. It's easy to get lost in it."

"Well, I'd like some time alone, at home in my own bed, so I can be away from all the business that goes on around here," Mr. Baumgartner quipped.

"I think that can be arranged," Daniel replied. He and Zoey approached the patient, who was sitting up ramrod-straight, playing solitaire on the bedside tray. Introductions were made and home care options were discussed. It was agreed that Zoey would see him in the mornings, around breakfast time, to fix his first meal of the day, lay out his daily meds and get him bathed and dressed. That would take her about an hour and a half, after which she would turn his routine daily care over to a hospice aid and do a quick call-in check on him later in the afternoon.

As it turned out, Mr. Baumgartner didn't want much fuss. In fact, his greatest goal was to maintain his independence for as long as he could. In spite of his seeming grumpiness right then, she was confident he would turn into a pleasant, cooperative patient once he had better control of his surroundings. Going home always made a significant difference.

"He seems so vital," she told Daniel a while later as they headed back to his office.

"He *is* vital, and while he's pretty sick right now, like I said to you earlier, I'm holding out some hope that we can actually take him out of hospice care sometime in the future."

"That would be amazing. I don't get to see many people graduate and move back into a normal life."

"It does happen, though, doesn't it?"

"Occasionally." She frowned and a sadness set into her eyes. "Not as often as I'd like to see, though."

"Then you get attached to your patients?"

"Of course I do. How can you invest part of every day in a person and not get attached?"

"You were attached to Elizabeth?"

"Very," she replied softly. "She was…exceptional."

"She was, wasn't she?"

Zoey reached over and squeezed Daniel's hand. "Very."

"I appreciate that."

It was like a heavy woolen blanket came down over them and stopped them from progressing in that moment. Both Daniel and Zoey stood in the hallway outside the elevator bank, thinking their own private thoughts about Elizabeth. It was a very long moment before Daniel finally spoke. "But not all your patients are as exceptional as Elizabeth was, are they?"

Zoey shook her head no, and laughed. "Some of them are real stinkers."

"What's the worst thing that ever happened to you with one of your stinkers?"

She didn't hesitate with her answer. "Bedpan to the chest. He hurled it across the room at me."

"It was empty, I hope?" The elevator doors opened and he stepped back to let Zoey enter ahead of him.

"Let's just say that, after I washed up, I threw those clothes away." Stepping into the elevator, she stopped at the button panel and pushed "2" to take them back to the second floor. The doors closed and they were alone for a long, quiet ride down. It was only when the doors opened to let them out that Daniel resumed the conversation.

"Can't say that's ever happened to me."

"Because you're a doctor," she said, laughing. "You don't get near bedpans."

"I beg to differ with you. I've seen my fair share of them."

"But how many people have you actually put on or taken off them? See, that's the real question here."

"Doctors aren't expected to do bedpan duty."

"Is that what they teach you in med school these days?"

"Not taught. Just implied."

"That's right. There's always this division of power, isn't there?" This was a fun conversation, a pleasant diversion from serious, sorrowful subjects. "Doctors hand out the orders, nurses do all the work."

"You're one of those?" he asked.

"You bet your life I'm one of *those*, and I'm proud to be a defender of nurses everywhere. Without us, you doctors would end up doing the bedpan thing, and don't you forget that!"

Daniel chuckled. "You're quite the militant, aren't you?"

"Not militant. More like determined."

They wandered down the hall, shoulder to

shoulder, until they came to his office. "Well, Nurse Determined, this is where I leave you, unless you'd like to come in for a few minutes?"

She looked over his shoulder at the door, but didn't take a step forward. "I… Um… Your office is so small. Are you sure I'd fit in there with you?" Such a lame reason for not stepping over his threshold. But she didn't want to go in, didn't want to get any more personal with him than she already had. And a tight space like his office, well, that had "togetherness" written all over it.

"Elizabeth never went in there, either. She'd bring me my lunch and stay ten paces back from the door after she knocked, because just seeing the size of my office almost caused a panic attack in her. But she never said a word about it."

"Not even to you?"

"I think especially not to me. Elizabeth was never good at letting anyone see or know about her weaknesses. People expected her to be strong—I expected her to be strong. And she was afraid that, if anyone perceived anything other than strength in her, she'd be letting them down."

"But you were aware enough of her to know her deep, dark secret."

Daniel smiled fondly. "I suppose I was. But I never let on."

"Because you loved her?"

"Because I respected her need to keep it to herself."

Zoey wondered how it would be to have someone so close to you that he'd simply know and understand all your intimacies without ever being told. That was Daniel and Elizabeth's marriage, though. A perfect love story. She envied that, and she also pitied the person who ever stepped into Daniel's life in the future, because he still held Elizabeth in such high esteem; no one could, or would, compare. Bottom line, for Daniel, Elizabeth was an act that probably couldn't be followed successfully.

"So you're sure you won't come in for a little while?" he asked, interrupting her thoughts.

"I don't think so."

"Is it because of claustrophobia, or me?"

"What do you mean *you*?"

"You're not comfortable around me. I can see it every time I look at you."

"I've no reason to be comfortable…or not comfortable." That wasn't exactly the truth, as she could see herself becoming very comfortable with Daniel, and very quickly at that. She was fighting it, though. Paddling upstream and struggling against the current every inch of the journey. And it wasn't because of Daniel as much as it was about her. She was afraid to take the journey. Afraid of being hurt again. Afraid of being so unaware of herself that she would allow herself to get hurt.

"Is it because of Elizabeth?"

She preferred not to answer his question, because she didn't understand why she reacted to Daniel the way she did. She liked him. Liked him a lot. But that didn't change the fact that her reactions toward him were not natural. Nor were they intended. Rather, they simply happened, and it didn't seem like she could hold them back. "It's because I'm just…cautious. That's my nature, I guess, when something out of the blue approaches me. And I've got to tell you, you're definitely out of the blue."

"Out of the blue and, apparently, out of practice, since all I want to do right now is ask you down to the cafeteria for coffee, and I don't know how to do it to get a positive response."

His directness caught her off-guard and she didn't know what to make of it. "Why?" she asked bluntly.

"Because you look like you could use a cup right about now."

"How do I look?"

"Apprehensive, distressed, maybe nervous."

Well, he'd nailed that description dead on. She was all three because Daniel signaled a moving forward in her that she wasn't sure she was ready for. "Or maybe I'm anxious to get on with my day."

"But, by your own admission, this was the last stop of your day."

"I could have plans for the evening." If only that were only true.

"Do you?"

"I've got a lot of paperwork to catch up on." A dull, unimaginative excuse to be away from him. But away was where she had to be, lest she got herself more involved than she already was. The problem was, Daniel was such a big conflict for her. He represented something she longed for, but couldn't have in him as he was still married to Elizabeth emotionally and spiritually. That was a warning sign if ever there was one. She couldn't go past a certain point with Daniel because he was still committed to what he'd had, which meant there was no reason to go forward with anything, because in the end she'd be going forward alone.

Alone was where she lived her life now, and she was used to it. So why take the risk to change things?

"Paperwork? That's all?" he asked.

She nodded slowly. "My workday usually

carries over into my evening. It's part of what I do."

"You don't mind that?"

"I'm used to it, so it's not really a matter of liking or disliking. And I knew that's what I was letting myself in for when I took the job, like you knew the kind of hours you would put in when you became a doctor."

"So how do I rescue you from a few of those minutes of that paperwork?"

She looked at the broad smile crossing his face and caught herself falling victim to those amazing dimples that accented either side of his mouth. "I suppose all you have to do is ask." The words tumbled out before she could stop them, and she immediately regretted that she'd sounded too easy. But she'd practically led him on, hadn't she? Maybe even led herself on, as well.

"And you'd say yes?"

"Truthfully, I'm not sure what I'd say."

"Then how about I ask you out for a pizza instead of coffee? We can go grab Maddie away from her grandmother, since I already promised her pizza tonight, then go down to Papa Giovanni's. They've got a great thin crust that practically melts in your mouth. And they give Maddie and me extra toppings."

"Sounds...tempting." Too tempting...and

she didn't mean the pizza. So what was she doing, getting ready to accept his offer? Was she being foolish? Giving in to something she knew couldn't really happen?

"Tempting, but not convincing?"

"Is this a date, Daniel? I need to clarify that, because I don't date families of patients, or former patients. That's a hard-and-fast rule in my life."

"A convenient one, too, I expect."

"What do you mean by that?" What was he seeing in her that caused him to think that?

"What I mean is, you intentionally keep yourself at a distance. You say it's a professional rule, but I wonder if it extends beyond that."

It did, but she had no reason to confess that to him. Daniel wasn't a friend. He was merely someone she knew, the extension of one of her former patients. And her rules applied to him. Or, at least, she was struggling to make them apply. "My rule extends to wherever I want to apply it."

"And you never make exceptions?"

"Exceptions lead to more exceptions, and pretty soon the rules go by the wayside. It can turn into a slippery slope if you let it."

"So, what happens if that slope does get too slippery? What does it do to you?"

"It disappoints me. Disillusions me. Hurts me. I think it's easier to stay away from that slope than risk getting on it and falling down."

"Well, I'm asking you out to dinner, not a slippery slope. That's all. And the evening comes only with a couple of slices of pizza and some very enthusiastic chattering from a three-year-old."

"It *would* be nice to see Maddie again," she conceded.

"Then you'll come?"

Zoey sighed. She was about to give in to something she didn't want, and there was no stopping her now. She was far past that point, as the word *yes* was already pushing its way out. "I suppose two slices and some chatter won't be such a big deal." She shook her head as he once more invited her into his office. "Instead, how about I meet you at Giovanni's in a little while?"

"Sounds good to me." Daniel glanced at his watch. "It's six thirty now. I think it'll take me about an hour to get out of here and get Maddie rounded up, so let's say we meet up at seven thirty. Will that work for you?"

This was a mistake, a big, *big* mistake. She knew it, but that wasn't stopping her. She wanted to go, wanted to spend a little more time with him. Wanted to take him out of the medical atmosphere and, well, maybe even relate to him as a friend.

Daniel…a friend? It was something to consider.

Of course, it *had* been a full year since he'd been a family member of one of her patients. So why not let up a little this one time? "That'll give me enough time to run home and feed my cat."

"You have a cat?" Daniel grinned at her. "I didn't figure you'd go in for that kind of commitment."

"I commit beautifully to cats. Just not to people."

"Why?"

"Cats don't let me down. People do. I find a certain safety in cats."

He laughed. "Then you're not on your way to being the eccentric cat lady who has thirty cats living in her apartment?"

"One cat is companionship. Thirty is a retreat from the real world. And, believe it or not, I like the real world, even though it scares me sometimes." She turned and headed back toward the elevators, but stopped a few feet down the hall and spun back to face him. "Tell Maddie I'm looking forward to seeing her again."

Daniel merely nodded, then slipped into his office and shut the door behind him.

"So what have I done?" she asked herself as she pushed the elevator call button. The door opened immediately and she stepped into the empty lift and slumped against its back wall for the one-story descent. "What *have* I done?"

# CHAPTER FOUR

WELL, AT LEAST she hadn't turned him down. That was a good thing. But had she accepted his offer only because she wanted to see Maddie again, or had he actually convinced Zoey to go out with *him*? An almost-date standing on its own merits.

Daniel glanced at the picture of Elizabeth still sitting on his desk, then reached out and lightly ran his fingers over it. One photo, such fond memories. And such pain. Several times over the past year he'd tried putting it away, but he never could bring himself to do it. Once, he'd got it all the way to his desk drawer but he'd stopped short of putting it inside, instead placing it right back in its usual spot next to Maddie's photo.

"So I've done it," he said to the image of his late wife. "I think I've taken that first step. It's difficult, though, and I don't even know if I'm going in the right direction. But I'm trying,

Elizabeth, and I'm not sure how I feel about it."
Was he numb? Or afraid of letting his wife go?
Was he moving ahead or being disloyal? "It's
a lot to think about," he said, sighing wearily
as he removed his white lab coat and hung it
on a wall peg. Then he glanced down at the
wedding ring he still wore, fingering it tenderly. Yes, it was a lot, indeed!

But, no matter. The deed was done. He'd
asked, Zoey had accepted and that was that.
One pizza and no strings attached. Oh, and
with Maddie there as the buffer. That was the
way he was going to have to think about it to
get himself through the evening without feeling an overwhelming guilt. *What the hell am
I doing?* A chance meeting at a coffee shop, a
hospital fundraiser, scheduling a professional
appointment—these were all one thing. But
to ask her out…to *blatantly* ask her out for
pizza…

That was something altogether different,
and now he was feeling…confused. Yes, that
was it. He was confused. Afraid to take the
first step, afraid to move away from what he
knew and had always counted on and move
toward the unknown. It was too different, and
there were times now when he hated anything
different.

* * *

"She's looking forward to seeing you," he told Maddie a little while later. "Do you remember Zoey coming to our house?"

Maddie shook her head no, but she was in that stage right now where she responded negatively to everything. So he had no way of knowing whether or not she actually remembered Zoey taking care of Elizabeth during those last few weeks of Elizabeth's life. In a sense, he hoped she didn't, as he did not want Maddie to have those images of Elizabeth and her illness as her only memories of her mother.

"Well, even if you don't remember her, I know you're going to like her. In the meantime, what do you want on your pizza tonight?"

"I don't like pizza," Maddie responded sullenly, folding her arms tightly across her chest. It had been a particularly rough night to pick her up as Maddie had wanted to spend all night with her grammy, and have pancakes and maple syrup for dinner. That was Maddie's plan, anyway, one that Abby had been quite happy to accommodate. Also, it was one he'd changed, and Maddie wasn't happy about that. Hence her grumpy mood.

"Pizza's not your favorite food anymore?"

He wanted to laugh at his daughter's attempt to control her world, but he knew that, as soon as the pizza was placed in front of her, her walls would come tumbling down. A three-year-old's sellout to pepperoni and cheese.

"I hate pizza!" she said. And she meant it for the moment.

"Then that means there'll be more for me to eat."

"You can't have my pizza, Daddy."

"Why not, if you don't want it?"

"Because it's mine." Her sullen face grew even darker. "And I want it!"

"And you're not going to share with me?"

That question caught Maddie off-guard and she didn't answer for a few moments. "You can have one bite," she finally conceded.

"Thank you for that, Maddie! I really appreciate it." She didn't respond to him, so he continued, "So, do you like pizza again? Even a little bit?"

"I don't know," Maddie answered him.

"Are you going to be nice to Zoey tonight?"

"I don't know."

And so went the conversation the rest of the way to Giovanni's. Daniel was grateful for it, though, as it kept his mind off what he was about to do. Guilt and pepperoni were never a good combination.

* * *

Once inside Giovanni's, Daniel headed right for their usual table, up front at the window. A server immediately rushed over with a booster seat for Maddie, and Giovanni himself poked his head out the kitchen door and waved to Daniel. "Your usual tonight, Danny boy?" he hollered.

"Maybe. But someone's joining me in a few minutes, so let's hold off and see what she wants."

"A date?" Giovanni called out, grinning from ear to ear. He was a short, round little man with bushy eyebrows and an eternal twinkle in his eyes. "Finally!"

"A friend from work," Daniel responded, finding it hard to vocalize the word *date*. "She's a nurse."

"A sexy one, I hope," Giovanni said, then ducked back into the kitchen.

Zoey sexy? He hadn't given it that much thought up until now but, come to think of it, she *was* sexy. Very sexy. So why hadn't he noticed that about her before? Probably because he wasn't ready. And why was he thinking about that now? Probably because he *was* ready.

Zoey sexy... She'd changed clothes, he noticed first off as she entered through Giovanni's front door, out of her everyday work scrubs into a pair of casually worn jeans and a slipover, white cotton sweater. Her hair was down, too. It was a pleasant look altogether, and he wondered if the men in Giovanni's were staring at her as appreciatively as he was. "You remember Maddie," he said as Zoey approached the table.

"Of course I do!" Zoey bent down to extend a hand to Maddie. But Maddie would have no part in it and, instead, clamped her arms tight across her chest as per usual, then looked at the floor.

"She's got a stubborn streak tonight," Daniel explained while the server stood by to take their order.

The smell of pizza permeated the entire room and the hushed tones of everybody eating all the pizza caused the tiny place to spring to life.

"Any reason in particular?" Zoey took her seat and swung her strappy purse over the back of her chair.

"It seems that Maddie made other plans with her grandmother and I came along and spoiled them. That's why she's mad at me and, by extension, probably you, too. Isn't that right, Maddie?"

"I wanted pancakes!" the child mumbled into her chest.

"But you're getting pizza like I promised you. Remember, we talked about that this morning?"

"I *wanted* pancakes," she countered.

"Well, we don't always get what we want, Maddie. And when you're older, you'll understand this." Sighing, he turned his frazzled attention to Zoey. "Do you like Giovanni's so far?"

"I've never been here before," Zoey commented, "But it seems nice. And the atmosphere is lovely." She was referring to the quaint red-and-white checkered table cloths and the empty bottles of wine turned into candle holders.

"I hadn't been here, either, until Elizabeth…" He stopped and smiled sadly, the full weight of being here with someone other than Elizabeth finally catching up to him. This had been Elizabeth's favorite restaurant, a place he'd enjoyed with his wife so many times over the years. And here he was now, with somebody else. It didn't feel right, but it also didn't feel as wrong as it could have, which surprised Daniel. What a difference this past year had made…a difference he hadn't even recognized until this very moment. "Well, anyway, you're in for a treat. Maddie and I come here probably once a week now—don't we, Maddie?"

Typically, she didn't answer, but instead gave her head an adamant shake: *no.*

"It's a phase," Daniel explained. "One I hope she outgrows pretty quickly."

"Sometimes we just don't feel like talking," Zoey said. "Isn't that right, Maddie?"

"No!" the child exclaimed loud enough that half the people in the restaurant turned their heads to look at her.

"Inside voice," Daniel warned. "Use your inside voice, Maddie. Like we've discussed."

Maddie sat motionlessly in her chair and didn't respond.

"Well," he finally said to Zoey, "It looks like the conversation is up to the two of us tonight, since Maddie has chosen not to participate." He smiled over at his daughter. "But we'll work it out, won't we, Maddie?"

True to her newfound stubbornness, Maddie shook her head no, and Zoey couldn't help but laugh aloud. "She's certainly a stubborn one."

"Worn with pride, I'm afraid." Daniel looked up and noticed that the waiter was still standing there patiently, waiting for their order. "We'll have a large thin crust, with pepperoni and extra cheese…" He glanced over at Zoey. "Is that OK with you?"

"Sounds good."

"Then that's it. Oh, and milk for Maddie, and…" He looked back over at Zoey. "Want to split a pitcher of beer?"

"Sure," she said enthusiastically. "But could we make it light?" she asked.

Light? For a moment, Daniel thought about asking Zoey if she was watching her weight, but judging from what he'd seen of her so far, and what he hadn't seen of her in a very literal sense, she didn't have an inch extra on her anywhere. In fact, Zoey had perfect curves in all the right places, something that he had noticed in spite of his futile attempts not to. Even now, just *thinking* about looking at her, a little knot of desire punched him right in the gut. "Um…you'll like the pizza," he said, struggling for something to get his mind off the obvious thoughts trying to invade it.

"That's what you told me."

Still grappling… "Did I tell you they have a nice thin crust here?"

Zoey nodded, smiling. "And that they give you extra toppings."

Well, so much for getting his mind off how attractive he thought Zoey was. It was time to admit it to himself. She *was* attractive. Particularly attractive. Was sexy, too. Caught his interest in a way he didn't want his interest being caught. "OK, well, I *know* I didn't tell you I've tried making pizza at home, but it's just not the same as Giovanni's and Maddie refuses to eat it."

"So what do you do about that?"

"Fix her whatever she wants. And, before you jump in and tell me that I shouldn't let my daughter control me that way, I know that's true. But it's tough maintaining the status quo when I'm away from her so much of the time." Now, finally, he was back on less shaky ground! No more untoward thoughts.

"At least she has her grandmother. My mother worked three jobs most of the time and she left me with different people every day. First one neighbor, then the next. Anybody who was available to look after me for a day."

"Why so many people?"

"Because she couldn't afford a regular day-care center, and the best she could do was hire people who didn't want a regular commitment but were open to making a few extra dollars. They were cheaper for her."

"And it worked out for you?"

"Most of the people who looked out for me were nice. But I always missed my mom. Always wanted to have a more regular schedule than I did, because it got so confusing going from person to person."

"Other than that, you had a normal childhood?"

"I wouldn't say it was normal but, looking back, at the time I thought it was the way things were supposed to be. Parents left their children behind. Although I wasn't neglected, Daniel. Not by any means. Because my mother made up for her absences when she got home. Sometimes, too much so, I think. Probably because she felt guilty about being away so often."

"I'll bet she didn't dote the way my mom did—still does—on Damien and me."

"I wouldn't call it doting so much as riding herd. Mom had strict rules I was expected to follow even when she wasn't there, and she convinced me that she'd know if I was breaking them even though she was gone. That was back when I thought my mother had superpowers."

"Ah, yes. Woman with a cape."

"The invincible cape that came out whenever it was necessary. The thing is, I was a true believer in my mother's magical powers to simply know what I'd been up to. I mean, I couldn't get away with anything, and it wasn't for a lack of trying. Because I tried, and I was quite a handful at times, running around with the wrong people, staying out later than I was supposed to, going places where I was forbidden to go."

"I can't imagine you being a wild child."

"Not wild so much as pushing my boundaries. Trying to see how much I could get away with."

"Did you get away with very much?"

"No at all. My mother had a way of just handling my antics. And so patient… Oh, my heavens, that woman was patient with me!" Zoey laughed, suddenly feeling better about coming here with Daniel. This wasn't going to be a difficult evening after all. Daniel's relaxed demeanor spoke to that. But she wondered if some of what she was seeing was being forced, as she noticed the nervous way his fingers fidgeted, and the occasional distant look that tried overtaking his eyes.

"If you weren't wild, then why were you always testing your mother?"

"Always trying to find a way to get attention, because my mother didn't have a lot of time for me."

"Like I don't have a lot of time for Maddie."

"Does she try to get your attention?"

"All the time. And I give it to her whenever I can, but it never seems to be enough. Which is why I think it's so easy for Abby to spoil her."

"Which leaves you feeling guilty."

"Guilty as hell," he stated.

"But you're a good father, Daniel. I can see it. And Elizabeth often talked about how good you are with Maddie. That gave her a lot of comfort."

He smiled sadly. "Sometimes I'm not sure I'm good enough, though."

"But you said it yourself—Maddie's going through a phase. She'll outgrow it in time, when her intellect catches up to her emotions."

"And in the mean time I—"

"Take it as it comes," Zoey interrupted. "That's all you can do. Oh, and trust that in the end, with your good parenting, Maddie will turn out wonderfully."

He chuckled. "Good parenting. Right. Lately, I've come to appreciate my parents' good parenting more than I ever did before. The things they had to put up with from Damien and me... We really put them to the test sometimes."

"So what kinds of things did you and you brother do?"

Daniel slowly curled his lips into a reminiscent smile. "Mostly boy things, like setting the neighbor's shed on fire."

"You were an arsonist?" She arched amused eyebrows. "For real?"

"Hey, I didn't strike the match, if that's what you mean."

"But you were there, aiding and abetting."

"I prefer to think of it as observing."

"And Damien...your twin, I think is what Elizabeth told me?"

"Older by seven minutes."

"What was he doing?"

"Checking to make sure there was nothing in the shed. We'd already scouted it out ahead of time, then we waited until the neighbors were gone and my parents were otherwise occupied. It was a Saturday morning...early. We announced that we were going to the park for a game of basketball. Made a big deal of it, actually, which probably had my parents suspicious right off the bat. Anyway, instead of the park, we sneaked into the neighbor's backyard and that's where Damien produced the fateful book of matches he'd stolen from the kitchen drawer."

"You didn't have matches, too?"

"At that point, I was still a good boy. My dad told me not to play with matches, so I didn't."

"Yet you expected to burn down a shed."

"Damien expected to burn down a shed. I expected to watch."

"So it was Damien who didn't follow the rules."

"He still doesn't."

"But he doesn't burn down sheds now, does he?"

"His pent-up energies are spent in the OR. My brother's one hell of a surgeon." Said with pride.

"So, back to the shed."

"Yes, the shed. It didn't go up at first. One match wasn't enough. So Damien gathered up some kindling…"

"While you watched him?"

"While I watched him."

"Were you always the inactive participant?"

"Usually. Although I'll admit that I spawned a good many of our bad ideas."

"Bad ideas for Damien to carry out."

Daniel chuckled. "Something like that."

"So why did he do it and you didn't?"

"I was afraid to try new things. Always was, and I'm afraid a part of that is still lingering in me. I resist change."

"Like Maddie does."

"It's a good thing she's got a lot of Elizabeth in her to even her out."

"Oh, I think you even her out, too. You

just don't realize that yet. Anyway, so you and Damien burned that shed to the ground. Right?"

"After our initial failure trying to get the fire to catch, it finally did, and when that happened there was no turning back. We had a full-fledged fire that was worthy of any junior league arsonist. Especially when that fire finally spread to the shed door, then to the front of the structure. Eventually the whole thing went up, and that's when my parents, followed by a bunch of firemen, showed up. By then the shed was a total loss and Damien and I knew we were in a world of hurt because of it."

"Ah, yes. The punishment phase."

"Which we hadn't thought through." Daniel smiled. "And, boy, was it rough. First we had to rebuild the shed, with our dad's help. Then we had to spend an entire summer in indentured servitude to our neighbors, which kept us away from pretty much all of our usual activities. Plus our parents added chores to our normal chore list."

"All of which kept you too busy to get into any more trouble." Zoey laughed. "Sounds like a brilliant plan to me."

"In retrospect, it was." He shook his head. "We learned our lesson and the junior arsonists never picked up a book of matches again."

He paused as the waiter moved in to set the pitcher of beer on the table.

"So, what if Maddie burns down a shed one day?"

"I'll send her down to my parents and let them deal with it. If they raised two hard-headed, often bad sons to be successful, I'm sure they'd be fine with one stubborn little girl." Daniel poured beer from the pitcher into two mugs then hoisted his own mug up to his mouth and took a sip. "That's supposing that people look at Damien and me as successful."

"That depends on how you define success, I suppose."

Daniel relaxed back into his chair, then scooted a sippy cup of milk in Maddie's direc-tion. "Good life, good family and friends, good job. That's all a person really needs. That, and maybe a cat!"

Zoey laughed. "Definitely a cat."

# CHAPTER FIVE

DANIEL SAT BACK on the green wooden park bench and watched Zoey push Maddie in the swing. Zoey was all smiles and Maddie was all giggles—something beautiful to watch. Something else beautiful to watch: Zoey in her little pink T-shirt. And her curves. Dear God, he was watching something that he really shouldn't. *Again!* Something that made him feel disloyal to Elizabeth. *Again!* But, try as he might, he couldn't take his eyes off her. Try as he might, he didn't *want* to take his eyes off her. Of course, he could chalk it up to the fact that most men admired beautiful women, and he fell into the category of most men.

Or he could admit to himself what he'd admitted the night before. He found Zoey particularly attractive. The way she moved, and smiled, and laughed…it was all so appealing. Damn it! That was an admission he didn't want to make. Didn't want to think about. Wasn't ready to admit to. But he couldn't turn it off.

So was this lonely desperation pulling him in, or was it a genuine attraction, like the attraction he'd felt for Elizabeth the first time he'd laid eyes on her?

Truthfully, he didn't want to know the answer, as his choices over what to do about it weren't exactly clear in his mind. *Just shut your eyes and clear your head, Daniel. Yeah, right*. Easier said than done.

"See how high I'm going, Daddy!" Maddie called out to him, thankfully breaking into his thoughts about Zoey.

"That's pretty high," he called back. She was barely off the ground, and strapped into a toddler's swing, but his daughter was feeling all grown up right now, and it was cute. In fact, it was so cute he took out his phone and recorded several seconds of video of Maddie and Zoey together, something he'd transfer to his computer and store along with all his other videos and pictures. The recorded history of Maddie's life that Elizabeth had wanted to give Maddie on her twenty-first birthday. One of Elizabeth's strongest wishes for her daughter that he'd made a promise to carry out.

For a moment, he imagined Elizabeth there, pushing Maddie on the swing. Elizabeth's long, blond hair was being tossed in the breeze and she was laughing. Such a beautiful laugh. Infectious. Musical. And Maddie looking so much like her mother it hurt.

Daniel shut his eyes to hold the memory in but, as he concentrated hard to keep it in place, it seemed to fade away anyway. And there he was again, watching Zoey. But this time not with attraction so much as admiration for all the qualities that were uniquely hers...qualities that were nothing like Elizabeth's.

Yes, asking Zoey to come to the park with them this morning had been difficult, as it signaled the first time he'd truly stepped away from Elizabeth and allowed him to see himself with another woman. But it was also definitely a good idea because he knew he needed to take that step.

Of course, it had taken a bit of persuasion on his part to get Zoey to agree to the outing. She was as reluctant to move forward as he was, and two reluctant souls put together didn't move forward at a very fast pace.

"I'm accepting only because I don't have to work," she'd cautioned him. "No other reason, Daniel."

So much difficulty in such a simple thing.

Now here they were, all three of them together, enjoying the day. Or, in Zoey's case, a couple hours of it, as that was all she'd promised him. And in spite of all his qualms over asking her, and there were many—all stemming from his feelings of guilt over a marriage that had been unfairly taken from him—he was glad he'd asked, as Zoey was a natural with Maddie. It was nice watching them together, although Daniel had to keep reminding himself that this was not his future. It was only part of the process of moving on, and Zoey was only a friend. And it should have been Elizabeth here instead.

*"Go on without me, Daniel..."*

Sighing, Daniel pulled himself off the bench and headed toward the swings. "You ladies ready to eat?" he called out to them, suddenly feeling a little drained from his emotional tug-of-war. Enjoying his day with Zoey. Hating his guilt over enjoying the day. Finding Zoey attractive. Hating himself for finding someone other than Elizabeth that attractive.

"Any time you are," Zoey called back enthusiastically.

"Well, I've packed a variety of things, so you've got some decisions to make."

"I want yogurt!" Maddie cried. "Strawberry."

"And I just happen to have strawberry yogurt with me," Daniel said, lifting his daughter from the swing. "I also brought string cheese. Which would you prefer?"

Maddie frowned, like she was on the verge of making the biggest decision of her life. "Can I have both?" she finally asked.

He arched eyebrows at Zoey and smiled. "I think we can manage that. Unless Zoey wants your yogurt and string cheese."

"Do you?" Maddie asked her shyly.

"Nope. Those sound like just what you need." Zoey fell in line behind Daniel as he and Maddie walked hand in hand toward the picnic table.

"She doesn't want them, Daddy," Maddie informed him in all seriousness.

Daniel picked up his daughter and swung her around and onto the picnic bench. Damn, he wanted to get himself back into the present, get Elizabeth out of his mind for a little while and replace her with what he was doing right now. But she was hanging on to him and not letting go…something he was beginning to regret. How long would this phase last? he wondered as he opened the picnic basket and set out a huge hand-tossed salad for Zoey and himself.

"Looks delicious," Zoey commented, taking her seat across from Maddie. "Is there anything I can do to help you?"

Still trying to block Elizabeth out, Daniel shook his head. "I kept this simple. When I was a kid, my parents would take Damien and me on picnics every now and then, and my mother would spend hours in the kitchen preparing for it. I always wondered how she could enjoy herself after all that work. So now, when Maddie and I go out, I grab whatever's handy, or buy something on the way, because I'd rather use the hours my mother spent cooking enjoying my daughter."

"Smart move. People get so tied up in things that aren't important, they miss the real point."

"Like food?" he asked. Daniel set the table with Maddie's lunch then took his place next to her.

"Is food really the object of a picnic, or is it about having fun and enjoying the people you're with?"

"I'm not much into food anymore. Elizabeth was a brilliant cook, and I ate well with her, but since she's been gone none of it seems to matter. I feed Maddie what she wants, which is very little, and I usually snack off that. So for me, food's never the object."

"You've picked up a few pounds, though." Zoey uncapped a bottle of water and took a drink.

"Does it look bad?" he asked.

She shook her head as she sat the water down on the table. "You were getting too thin, I think. It's understandable, and I see that happen to family members all the time. But you do look better now."

He smiled, surprised and even pleased that Zoey had observed that about him. "I need to keep fit for Maddie's sake."

"And for your own, Daniel. You count in that equation, too, you know."

"Is that what you tell all the families?"

"I never go on picnics and get this involved with my families."

"But you've made the exception with me." He was flattered.

"I have, and I still don't understand why."

"No explanations necessary. I'm just glad you agreed to come with us today." He looked down at his daughter, who was smeared with yogurt up to her ears. "I think Maddie's glad, too. Aren't you, Maddie?"

Maddie nodded, her sticky face all set in concentration on the eating task at hand. Zoey handed Daniel a face towel to take care of Maddie's mess. "She's doing better than she did the other night when we went out for pizza. I was afraid after that, that she wasn't going to warm up to me."

"It takes her a little while, but she eventually gets there." He tousled his daughter's hair. "Anyway, are you up to a museum or something else after we eat?"

"I don't think so. I do have some paperwork to catch up on later today, and I need to make a few phone calls."

Daniel hadn't expected any more from Zoey, but he'd asked anyway. "Some other time, then?" he asked, not sure whether he sounded hopeful or wary.

"Maybe," she said cautiously.

"Depending on what?" Daniel asked, venturing a step forward. One of the steps Elizabeth had asked of him.

"I'm not sure. Being here with you and Maddie like this isn't something I normally do, and I need to see how I am with it once I'm by myself."

"We're that big of a step for you?" Apparently, she had her own steps to take, too.

"You have no idea. I set these fixed standards and it's not like me to go against them. But all the rules I made were broken because I made the exception for you, and it's not sitting as right as I'd like it to. And I apologize if my being so honest offends you, but I think it's only fair to let you know how I'm feeling, since it concerns you."

"I appreciate the honesty." *If not the sentiment.*

She shrugged. "We'll see, OK?"

"OK," he agreed. "And in the meantime, if you change your mind, Maddie and I are at the other end of the cell phone. Call us if you find that your afternoon plans don't come off as you'd expected. Or you simply want to change them."

Zoey pushed herself off the bench and stood alongside the table for a moment. "Look, I've enjoyed this. The food was excellent and the conversation very nice."

"But you're writing us off anyway?" he asked, also standing up.

"It's time. But I don't want you to think I'm ungrateful or anything since I'm leaving. Because I'm not. This has been lovely."

"Do I scare you, Zoey?" he asked bluntly. "Or is it the situation between us that scares you?"

"You don't scare me, Daniel. Neither does our situation. I'm just trying to be a little more aware of what I'm doing. It's easy to say yes to you, because I do like you and I enjoy being with you, but yes isn't always in my best interests."

"What's in your best interests, Zoey? Tell me. Because I want to look after that, too."

"Well, for one, it's keeping away from things I know can hurt me."

"You think I can hurt you?"

"Not intentionally. But I don't want to get too invested in you only to find out that you can't get that invested in me. That was my marriage and, if it's taught me one thing, it's not to put myself into a position where I'm going to be left standing alone at the outcome. When I went into my marriage to Brad, I did so with all kinds of hopes and dreams, only to discover that hopes and dreams won't be fulfilled if the person you're with doesn't, or can't, reciprocate them." She shrugged. "My walls are well-constructed, Daniel. I don't want to go through that again."

"So it's all about self-survival?"

Zoey laughed. "That sounds so serious."

"It is, but we all have the instinct. Yours just seems to be a little more acute than most."

"Years and years of practice."

"So what are we going to do about that?" he asked.

"*We* aren't going to do anything, Daniel. There is no *we*. And *I'm* not going to do anything at the moment because I don't think you're ready to move forward yet. Also, I'm not ready to compete in an arena where the last contender was perfect."

She'd actually thought of herself in terms of competing with Elizabeth? That surprised him, and flattered him, as well. "Do you feel like I'm putting you in the position to compete with her? Because I don't intend to."

"It's not that you're putting me there, so much as *I* feel like I'm in the position to have to compete. And maybe I wouldn't feel this way if I hadn't known Elizabeth. Or if you'd been a widower with a wife I'd never met. But I knew Elizabeth. Knew her very well, as a matter of fact. And I know I can't hold a candle to her."

"Nobody's asking you to."

"No. Nobody is. But that doesn't stop me from feeling like I'd always come in second place. You've had your great love, Daniel, and I don't know that you can ever be truly happy with anything that comes afterward."

"Can I do something to change that? Do something to help you get through it?"

"Do I need to get through it?" she asked him. "I mean, really, if we're not involved, can't I just live with my feelings?"

"But we *are* involved, Zoey. Like it or not, and fight it as hard as you wish, but we've been involved in one way or another since that day at the coffee shop. I'm not quite sure how, yet, but it's there."

"So is Elizabeth."

"Which I can't change. She was…still is…a very important part of my life, and I'm not making any apologies for the way I feel about her. She's always going to be with me, through Maddie, through my memories… We didn't divorce, like you did when your love ended. We ended in love."

"And that's my problem to deal with, Daniel. Not yours."

"That's where you're wrong. See, it's my problem, too."

"How?"

"I like having you in my life. Like having you as a friend. Like the idea that we could become more than friends at some point. But with Elizabeth being your stumbling block…" He shrugged. "I don't know how to go about this, Zoey. You know I haven't dated. I hadn't even thought about dating again until you."

"But I'm scared to be your first, Daniel. I don't want to be the *practice* date for something or someone else you might find on down the line."

"That's direct." More direct than anything he'd ever had with Elizabeth, and he found it nice. Refreshing. Something he hadn't known he'd missed out on until he found it in Zoey.

"Well, we *are* direct, aren't we? But we're also honest. I mean, I know we're flirting with something, Daniel. I can feel it, and I think you can, too. It's so undefined, though, and I'm not sure either one of us wants to define it."

"So what's the next step here?" This was confusing him. She was as much as admitting that she had feelings for him, yet she was running away from them. Of course, he wasn't exactly advancing that far forward, either, was he? And, deep down, did he even want to advance?

Zoey reached across and squeezed his hand. "You'll know what you have to do when the time is right."

"I hope so."

"I know so." She stepped back from the table. "Like I said, I do appreciate being asked to come out with you today. It's nice doing something different for a change."

"Will I see you again?" he asked, in spite of his misgivings.

"How about we leave it as it is for now, and I'll call you later in the week to let you know how Mr. Baumgartner is doing with home care?"

"Be warned—I might suggest something then." If he screwed up the courage.

"And I might be agreeable." She looked down at Maddie, who was disassembling her stick of string cheese. "I'll see you soon, Maddie. It was fun playing with you today."

Maddie nodded but didn't look up. But Daniel waved at Zoey as she trekked off to her car. It *had* been a nice morning. A bit of an eye opener, as far as Zoey's openness was concerned. At least he knew where he stood. Nowhere, was the answer, and he should have been satisfied with that, given his own conflicted feelings. But he wasn't. Not at all. The only thing was, he wasn't sure if he was up to pursuing her just now. His life was full, and it would probably be best to stick to what he already had. He was perfectly contented there.

Still, Zoey was stirring things up in him. Things that hadn't been stirred in a very long time. He couldn't determine what or how yet, but he felt the gentle nudges, trying to let themselves in, which meant it was time for some deep soul-searching. Of course, that was some thinking best put off until another day. Right now, he had to concentrate on Maddie and what the two of them were going to do with the rest of their day.

Anything to put it off, he thought to himself as he cleared the picnic table. Definitely, anything to put it off.

* * *

Zoey didn't turn back to wave at Daniel and Maddie as she took the walk to her car. She could feel his eyes burning into the back of her, however, and she really wanted to have a look to see if he was staring, or if her imagination was working overtime. But she resisted temptation and walked on, wondering what she was going to do. Daniel obviously wanted something from her, or had expectations of her, and maybe she was sending out signals that were inviting him in. She didn't know... She didn't think she was, but it was clear Daniel was reading something.

"No, I don't have a boyfriend yet," she told her mother a little while later. That was the truth, but her mind did wander back to Daniel and, for a moment, she thought about telling her mother about him. Only a moment! Then the urge left her. "I'm still doing the same thing. Nothing's changed."

"You're not getting any younger, Zoey," her mother warned.

Zoey held out her cell phone and frowned at it, not that her mother would sense that frown all the way back in Omaha. But it made Zoey feel better. "My life is good the way it is." As she spoke the words, though, she wasn't as convinced as she normally was.

"You don't want to make it better?"

"I thought Brad would make it better, and look what happened there." Her mother had loved Brad. But Brad had disappointed her, too, as for a time, she'd thought him to be the perfect man.

"That was unfortunate. He wasn't who we thought he was."

"No, he wasn't. When I first met him I thought he was wonderful, and if anybody had told me he would drain my bank account, or cheat on me, I wouldn't have believed them."

"He fooled both of us, dear. But you're strong. You'll get over it."

"I *am* over it, Mother." Even with all the talk of Brad swirling around her, Zoey's mind raced back to Daniel. She liked his manly looks, his manly charms. Apparently her tastes had changed drastically since Brad, and for that she was glad. Daniel gave her an awareness that she welcomed, and he also gave her the hope that sometime, in the future, she could completely step away from her past.

"Don't get me wrong, Zoey. I'm on your side. I'm always on your side, which is why I worry about you so much."

"No need to worry, Mother. I'm doing just fine." She said that wistfully, as she was beginning to understand that there was something beyond *just fine* for her.

Daniel looked at the caller ID on his phone and saw that it was Zoey calling him. Today was Thursday and he hadn't seen her since Sunday. But he'd thought about her these past few days. Probably too much.

The phone continued to ring and, for an instant, the excitement stirred in him. But he tamped it right back down when he realized that this had to be the call about Mr. Baumgartner. "Oh, well..." he said as he hit Answer.

"Can we meet in person, Daniel?" was the first thing she said to him. Not "hello," or "how are you doing?" or any other pleasantry. No, Zoey led right in with business.

"Is this about Mr. Baumgartner?" he asked.

"Yes. But I don't want to go into it on the phone. It's too complicated."

Now he was puzzled. "I have a light afternoon. Want to meet at the coffee shop?" That was neutral territory, and he assumed she'd be all into a neutral meeting.

"Or I could come to the hospital, if that would be better."

"Suit yourself," he said, trying not to sound too anxious.

There was a slight hesitation on her end, then she finally said, "I'm headed into my office to pick up some supplies, so how about I stop in the hospital afterward?"

"And brave my tiny office?"

"I haven't had my wrestling match with cramped spaces today, so I'm probably due."

"Then I'll see you in a little while. Call me when you get here." He waited for her to say goodbye, or something personal, but instead she merely hung up. Dead silence. No pleasantries again. "So, Zoey…"

He sighed as he walked down the hall to Room Three-Eleven. His patient there was a young woman diagnosed with an ovarian cyst. It wasn't serious, but she was falling apart at the prospect of surgery, and he'd been asked in to check her out and possibly prescribe a mild sedative.

Pulling on the requisite latex exam gloves, he stepped in the room and smiled. "Hello," he said. "I'm Dr. Caldwell. I hear you're not feeling so well, so let's see what we can do about that…"

A little while later Daniel was strolling down the hall on his way to his next patient when Zoey phoned. "I'm on my way over right now," she told him.

"I'll be back at my office in about half an

hour, after I finish my exam here, then do the charting." He liked hearing her voice. Liked it that she called him. In fact, when her name had come up on his caller ID, his heart had skipped a beat.

"I'll be waiting," she said, then hung up.

"She sounded sexy," a man in a wheelchair said, coming up on him from behind.

Daniel spun around to face him, surprised that the man was so close to him. Had he been so caught up in his moment with Zoey that everything else had escaped him? "You could hear her?"

"You had the phone turned to speaker. And, if I were you, I'd get on down to your office. You don't want to keep the lady waiting too long."

No, he didn't want to keep her waiting too long, but that was what it seemed like he was doing in so many ways. Taking a step forward, then retreating. Hesitating. Asking, then fearing the answer... Yes, in so many ways.

"You're going over to see *him*?" Sally McCall, Zoey's office manager, asked. Sally was a decade older than Zoey, an attractive woman with four children and a doting husband. Over the course of the year that Sally had worked at Home Health Care, they'd become friends of sort. Not close friends, so much as proximity friends. "The same one I've heard you talking to on the phone? The same one who causes you to sigh after you hang up with him?"

"No, I'm going over there to consult on a mutual patient. I called him and set up an appointment because Mr. Baumgartner dismissed us for no good reason this morning, and I thought Daniel… Dr. Caldwell…should know."

"And you couldn't tell him on the phone?"

"I could have," Zoey defended, "But I have some other concerns I want to address with him, and that's best done face to face."

"Well, I haven't seen this Dr. Caldwell face to face, but I'm betting it's a handsome face, or else you wouldn't be so anxious to get over there and see him."

"You sound like my mother."

"If your mother sounds like someone who would love to see you happy, then I take that as a compliment."

"Look, Sally, Daniel's a nice man. I like him and, yes, I've sort of been on the edge of going out with him. But I nursed his wife a year ago, before you came to the agency, and he's not over her. So, until he lets her go, nothing's going to happen."

"Is he worth the wait?"

That was a good question—a question that plagued Zoey for the rest of her time in the office and on into her walk over to the hospital. Was Daniel worth the wait?

While he waited for Zoey to show up, Daniel checked on a patient with pneumonia and one with chronic leg cramps, made two phone calls to verify various tests results and charted his notes for several patients. All in a day's work, he told himself, as he got so caught up in what he was doing he almost forgot that Zoey was on her way to see him. So, as he was punching into the nurses' station computer the last of his new orders, he glanced up and was actually caught off-guard when he saw Zoey approaching. Such elegance in motion, he thought, enjoying the full view of her. "Am I late for our appointment?" he asked her when she stopped directly across the desk from him.

"Actually, I'm a little early," she said, her lips curving into a warm smile.

"Well, I'm done here, and I don't have anything scheduled for the next couple of hours, so I'm all yours." In any way she wanted him. "So, what do I need to know about Mr. Baumgartner?"

She fished a note from the black binder she was carrying and laid it on the nursing station desk for Daniel to see. "This is what he left for me today."

Daniel picked it up and read it, the frown on his face growing deeper the further into it he got. Finally, "He's dismissed you?"

"And you, apparently. He said he doesn't want anymore medical attention from anyone."

"You've talked to him since I have. Did he leave any hints why?"

Zoey shook her head. "He seemed fine yesterday. Eager to get along with his various treatments. Overall optimistic outlook, as far as I could tell."

"Did you see him at all today?"

"No. After I read the note I decided not to go inside. He made it perfectly clear he doesn't want me, or anybody else, helping him."

"Damn! And I thought he was going to do well, being at home." Daniel reached up and shoved his hair back from his face. "I wouldn't have dismissed him from the hospital so soon if I'd known he'd do something like this."

"Well, you can't force it on him, Daniel. The man's pretty set in his ways."

"Ways that will kill him."

"Which he understands. I mean, you've made sure he knows everything he should know about his condition, and I've stressed that if he does well and follows all your orders we might be able to take him out of hospice care and turn him over to general home care, provided we see significant improvement. We've *both* told him it's possible he might not die for quite some time. So, other than that, what could we have done differently?"

"To be honest, probably nothing. Some patients think they know more than we do."

"And some patients just give up. Anyway, I wonder what he'll do," Zoey said.

"Get a damned house call from me, that's what!"

"Seriously? You'd go there?"

"No reason not to."

"Except the obvious one—he's dismissed all of us. Oh, and you're a hospitalist, and hospitalists work exclusively in a hospital."

"Well, I'm about to make myself the exception to that. Also, I'm not dismissed until Baumgartner tells me directly."

She smiled at him. "You're a good doctor, Daniel. There aren't too many of your sort who would make that house call these days."

He saw the sincerity in her eyes and it tweaked his heart. Compliments were always nice, but this one seemed especially nice coming from Zoey. So, why did it matter so much?

Daniel thought about that for a moment, then fought off the urge to ponder anymore.

There wasn't any point. She'd made it perfectly clear that she intended to remain at a distance. Like Mr. Baumgartner, she'd made her choice.

"Can I come with you?" she asked.

That surprised him. Zoey was the one who officially didn't want to get involved, yet here she was involving herself in something she really didn't have to. Impressive, he thought as he nodded his acceptance. "Sure. If you've got the time."

"Good. Then let me run across the street, throw a couple of things Mr. Baumgartner might need—if he decides to have us back—into my medical bag, and I'll be ready to go."

"That'll give me time to let my med students know I'll be out for a couple of hours, so they can cover for me."

"Can I ride with you?"

"Sure. Especially since we have to come back here afterward." And most especially since more time alone with Zoey was an exciting prospect.

"Good. Then I'll see you in a few minutes. I'm right across the street in the Tower Building, Suite Two-Twenty. Ask for me at the desk."

"See you in a few," he said, heading out to his office, telling himself every step of the way, *This is not a date.* But, *damn!* Why was he as excited as if it were? And why wasn't Elizabeth's image plaguing him with guilt the way he expected…maybe even the way he wanted? What was this? Was he finally moving on? Did he want to? Could he do it?

God help him, *would* he do it?

# CHAPTER SIX

THE RIDE TO Mr. Baumgartner's house was particularly quiet. So much so that Zoey actually felt a little uncomfortable sitting in the front seat next to a very still Daniel. He talked about work occasionally, and primarily focused on topics that elicited only a yes-or-no answer from her, which didn't exactly give her a prime opportunity to participate in the conversation. Thankfully, the trip took only ten minutes—a *long* ten minutes, though.

"Has he been your patient long?" she finally asked once they turned off the main drag onto a side street that led straight to Baumgartner's house.

"He was admitted three weeks ago, and that's the first time I met him. He'd asked me to follow him, though, and I was going to do that through our clinic."

"So why isn't his family doctor looking after him now?" She really wanted get off the topic, but Daniel didn't seem to want to steer the conversation in any other direction.

"He didn't have a family doctor. In fact, he told me he hadn't seen a doctor for anything in more than ten years."

"Ten years? That's crazy!" Crazy, maybe, but so many of her patients told her the same thing. They didn't go then, when they finally did, it was too late.

"Some people hate doctors. Or are afraid of them. I think he was one of them. Or maybe he's just plain negligent and doesn't care about his health." Daniel frowned. "Which explains why he's in the condition he's in. Congestive heart failure is fatal if left untreated, and he's had it—untreated—for a while."

"While I know he's classified as end stage, he doesn't necessarily have to die from it right now, if you can keep it under control. See, that's what I don't understand. Mr. Baumgartner has a lot riding on the care he's receiving, yet he's refusing it. If any of my other patients were given the least little bit of hope like he was, they'd do whatever they had to in order to hang on a little longer." She thought about Elizabeth and how fiercely she'd fought for more time with Daniel and Maddie. Daniel had to be thinking the very same thing, too. So, after being on the patient's end of it, how could he treat someone like Mr. Baumgartner who was refusing to join in the fight for his life?

Maybe it all boiled down to one thing: Daniel was an exemplary man.

"It happens, Zoey. I see it all the time. People make the choices they do for reasons I probably would never understand."

"You're too patient," she said.

"Years of practice."

"Well, I've had years of practice, too, and I still get frustrated."

"Because you can't control the situation?"

She laughed. "Because I can't control *me*."

"Ah, the wild spirit in the lady takes over."

"Well, that wild spirit is not always an attribute I admire."

"Are you going to unleash it on Mr. Baumgartner?"

"What I'm going to do is keep my mouth shut and let you do all the talking. Let's call it a case of the nurse deferring to the doctor."

"And you don't like to defer, do you?"

"Not usually. But today I'll make the exception."

"Elizabeth said you were fiery."

"She saw that in me? Because I really try to hide it when I'm with my patients."

"She was a perceptive lady who saw things other people couldn't. That's how we met, actually. She was visiting a friend in the hospital and, even though her friend said she was feeling OK, Elizabeth read the situation differently. So she came down to the nurses' station and practically dragged the first doctor she saw down to the room."

"That doctor would have been you."

He nodded. "And, as it turned out, Elizabeth was right. Her friend was on the verge of a diabetic crisis."

"Then the two of you fell in love immediately?"

"Actually, it took a couple of dates. But those came up in the first week we knew each other, and we were married two months later."

She glanced at his eyes and saw a trace of sadness take them over. There was no way she could measure herself against his memories. No reason to try. So she settled back into quietness for the rest of the ride.

It wasn't but a couple minutes later that Daniel slowed the car, flipped on the right-hand blinker then turned into a long, straight driveway leading up to a tiny white-framed house. Its yard was overgrown with trees and shrubs, and in the garden directly beneath the front window stood a collection of weather-beaten, blue-bodied, red-hatted gnomes. Overall, the house had a disheveled look to it. Not tidy at all. In fact, neglected throughout the years. "I don't think Mr. Baumgartner's much into yard work," she commented as Daniel stopped the car directly adjacent to the front walkway. "But the good news is, the inside of his house is better than this." Only because she'd had a cleaning crew come in her first day there.

"He told me his wife left him five years ago, so I guess that explains the lack of care. She was probably the one who saw to those things."

"She must have been the glue that held him together."

Daniel nodded. "The glue that ran off with a man twenty years her junior."

"He never told me that."

"Probably because it's not one of the best moments in his life."

"Well, I know how it feels to be cheated on, so I understand where he's coming from." Embarrassment, heartache, anger... Yes, she and Mr. Baumgartner probably did have something in common. "So, now that we're here, what's the plan?"

"How about we knock on the door and hope he opens up for us?"

"Not very likely, Daniel. Remember what that note said about not wanting to see any of us again?"

"That was then, this is now. He might have already changed his mind, or at least had some second thoughts. So, did you try to get in earlier? I'm assuming you have a key."

"I *did* have a key, but I turned it in at the office already, and they're going to take care of returning it to Mr. Baumgartner."

"You turned it in that fast?"

"Yep. Once we're dismissed from a patient, the supervisors don't let us hang onto any of his or her personal property. And that includes the house key. Which means that, if he doesn't answer his door, we're not going in."

Daniel sighed heavily. "Then let's hope he opens up." With that he climbed out of the car and hurried around to open Zoey's door for her. "Because if he doesn't, this was a big waste of time. Of course, we could always go to the coffee shop…"

"You and your coffee shop!" Daniel was finally beginning to loosen up, and she liked that. When he wasn't so guarded, he was very personable. Of course, he was personable when he *was* guarded, but it was a different kind of personable—the kind where he was pleasant enough to be around but you didn't give him a second thought. When he wasn't guarded, though, well…that set her toes to tingling. Which was invasive, took up too many of her thoughts, completely overwhelmed her when she let it. And that was a good summation of Daniel—sometimes he made her tingle, sometimes he did not.

Today, he was on verge of doing both to her, which left her feeling confused. "He's not going to answer his door," she said after Daniel's second knock.

"Maybe not," Daniel said, pulling back the screen door. He tried the doorknob and it gave to let them enter. So, they pushed on into the house and stopped just inside the door. "Mr. Baumgartner?" Daniel called out. "It's Dr. Caldwell from the hospital. I came to check on you."

No answer.

"I don't like this," Zoey whispered. "It's not right to just walk in."

"It's not right to ignore him, either." Daniel took a few steps into the living room then stopped. "Mr. Baumgartner?" he called. "Are you here?"

Again, no answer.

"I think we should go now," Zoey prompted from behind Daniel. This made her nervous. It almost made her feel like a burglar, and if not for Daniel being there with her, and actually leading the way, she would have been long gone.

"I think we should take a look in his bedroom," Daniel stated. He headed toward the hall but turned to Zoey before he proceeded down it. "You don't have to go if you don't want to."

Zoey blinked twice, then hurried to get behind him. "You're not leaving me here alone!" she whispered, almost bumping into Daniel in her haste.

"I'm coming in, Mr. Baumgartner. Along with Nurse Evans. We're both concerned about you."

This time when no answer came, Daniel picked up his pace on his way down the hall, and stopped short of entering the bedroom. There, in the doorway, lay a very unconscious man, amid a scatter of spilled pills. "Suicide!" Daniel whispered, dropping immediately to his knees in front of the man and feeling his neck for a pulse.

"Anything?" Zoey asked, also dropping down.

"A weak pulse." Daniel shook his head. "Call nine-one-one."

Zoey reached into her pocket and pulled out her cell phone as Daniel did a cursory exam on Mr. Baumgartner, checking his breath sounds and his eyes.

"He's not fixed and dilated," he said, looking up to Zoey. "But his breathing is irregular and shallow."

Zoey told the emergency dispatcher the address and urged them to hurry, then grabbed up the empty pill bottle on the floor next to her unconscious patient. "This was almost full yesterday," she told Daniel as she counted the pills scattered about. "I'm guessing he took about a dozen of these."

It was heart medication Daniel had prescribed. The right amount helped, the wrong amount brought about seizures, unconsciousness…death.

"Damn!" Daniel growled. "I completely missed all the signs."

"What signs?" Zoey asked. "I've been here every day this week and I never noticed anything off with him."

"He tried to kill himself, Zoey! That's about as *off* as it gets."

"But he didn't succeed."

"He would have, if we hadn't come here when we did. And he still may get his way, depending on how long the pills have been in him."

Zoey looked around the room and saw a cereal bowl sitting next to the bed. "He ate this morning, which tells me he wasn't anticipating committing suicide then. So he took the pills sometime after breakfast."

Daniel took Mr. Baumgartner's pulse again. "It's fading," he muttered, shaking his head in frustration.

"And there's nothing we can do," Zoey stated.

"He needs his stomach pumped, we need to get him on a cardiac monitor and have a ventilator on standby...and we're not exactly equipped to do all that here."

"So we wait for the ambulance." She reached across and squeezed Daniel's hand. "He's going to pull through this, Daniel. We got here in time to save him."

"But from what? The man was under hospice care. I don't imagine he could see much of a future for himself."

"But you told him that it may not be that bleak, that you could anticipate a recovery of sorts, depending on how hard he wanted to work for it."

"Well, apparently, he didn't want to work that hard." For a lack of anything better to do, Daniel felt Baumgartner's pulse again. He tried his neck, then his wrist, back to his neck. Then laid his hand on the man's chest to count breaths. But his hand didn't move, and nowhere he tried gave up so much as a twitch. Immediately he went up on his knees and assumed a position over his patient. "Arrest," he said, going in for the first chest compression.

Zoey raised up and tilted Mr. Baumgartner's head back, ready to start mouth-to-mouth. "Count it out," she urged Daniel, then waited until he announced thirty before she gave Mr. Baumgartner two deep breaths through an emergency breather she'd pulled out of her medical bag.

They repeated the procedure over and over, for the next five minutes, until the ambulance arrived. "Full arrest," Daniel told the paramedic. "We need to intubate and get an IV started before we take him in."

Zoey took the IV tubing and catheter from the paramedic and started the line herself as the paramedic took over the breathing duty. "What next, Daniel?" she asked, even though she could anticipate what he would want used.

"Give me one milligram of epinephrine, or ten millimeters of a one-to-ten-thousand solution. We'll keep it dripping in every three to five minutes while we're resuscitating him, hopefully following it up with a twenty milliliter flush when he's back." He continued his cardiac compressions. "*If* he comes back."

Zoey looked up at the second paramedic in the room, who was readying the endotracheal tube for Daniel. "When you get that done, bring in the stretcher. We need to transport him as soon as we can."

The paramedic, a young man with black, curly hair and an unusually large mustache, nodded and handed the tube and laryngoscope to Daniel. "I'll let the hospital know we're on the way in," he said, then hurried out.

"Need any help in there?" an emergency medical technician asked from the doorway. He'd shown up with the rescue squad from the fire department and, all in all, the house was filling up with medical help quite quickly. Since Mr. Baumgartner didn't want medical help anymore, she imagined he'd hate all this attention going on around him.

Daniel nodded his head. "Take over the compressions while I intubate."

The med tech followed Daniel's orders and was immediately on his knees, ready to take over where Daniel left off.

In the span of the thirty count, while she waited to breathe again for Mr. Baumgartner, Zoey studied Daniel's face—a beautiful face, she decided as he bit down on his lower lip in concentration. A face she could get used to if she allowed herself. "Hand me the bag," she said to a paramedic who was hovering over her, referring to the bag that would force breaths into Mr. Baumgartner's lungs once the endotracheal tube was in place.

"Is he resistant?" Daniel asked as he slid the tube into place so easily it looked like second nature to him.

"His breathing?" She shook her head. "No, his lungs aren't stiff at all."

"Any attempts at breathing on his own?" he asked once the cardiac monitor was in place and he was able to observe Mr. Baumgartner's wavering heart pattern.

"Afraid not."

"Well, I think we need to bundle him up and get him to the hospital anyway. There's only so much we can do for him here, and I'd rather finish this in the emergency room."

"Is he going to…?" She glanced across at Daniel, whose face was set in stone.

Daniel's eyes softened for a moment as he looked back at her. "I'm hoping for the best, but it's too soon to tell."

A lot of people would have given up on Mr. Baumgartner—a man with a potentially terminal illness who'd tried to take his own life. But Daniel was determined to pull him through, and she loved that in him. Admired it. Admired the way he cared about his patient, no matter what the condition.

"You do good work," she told Daniel. That

was an understatement, if ever there was one. Daniel did brilliant work and she was so proud of him, she could almost burst. What she'd witnessed here today was nothing short of a miracle—bringing a dead man back to life. Mr. Baumgartner was by no means out of danger yet, but she trusted Daniel to pull him through this crisis. More than that, she was coming to realize that she simply trusted Daniel...with everything.

Daniel glanced out the back window of the ambulance to make sure Zoey was following in his car. Glad to see her right behind them, he turned his attention back to his patient, and frowned. "I don't know what possessed you to do this, Mr. Baumgartner, but when you're conscious again we're going to talk about it." Had his patient died of an overdose, Daniel would have taken that as a personal failure. He should have seen it coming. Should have noticed that the man had been too euphoric in his grave condition. Thank God Zoey had brought him the note he'd left posted on his front door. If not for her quick thinking, Mr. Baumgartner wouldn't have pulled through.

She was a good nurse. A damned good nurse, which was a fact that hadn't escaped him when she'd been caring for Elizabeth.

Elizabeth had looked forward to Zoey's visits, had been genuinely happy to see her. They'd grown close over the course of weeks, and Daniel regretted now that he hadn't really been a part of that relationship. He'd missed out.

"They're transferring him to the ICU," he told Zoey a little while later as they walked out of the emergency room and headed to the elevator leading to the intensive care unit. The afternoon was long over by now, and it was well into the full of the evening, where the halls were thinning of guests and excess medical personnel. In essence, the hospital was getting ready to bed down for the night, and in its emptiness the clicking of Zoey and Daniel's heels on the beige tile floor in the hall was the only sound being made, except for the occasional ding of the elevator.

Zoey pushed the elevator down button and stepped back. "Has he come around yet?"

Daniel shook his head. "Not yet, but his vital signs are stable now, and I'm pretty sure we got most of the drugs pumped out of his system. So I'm optimistic."

"And he lives to try it again?" she asked.

Sadly, that was a distinct possibility. But, the next time Daniel dismissed him from the hospital, he was going to make sure Mr. Baumgartner had a psychiatric consult first.

"It's hard to predict. Some people want to extract every bit of life they can hang on to." Elizabeth, for example. "Some people simply don't care, though. I didn't think Mr. Baumgartner would be one of those."

The elevator doors opened and Daniel stepped back to allow Zoey to enter first. He followed her in, and intended to turn to face the door as it closed, but Zoey fell into his arms and laid her head against his chest. "I don't do resuscitations, Daniel. Haven't done one in years. Not in my specialty."

"Are you OK?" he asked her, pulling her tighter into him and leaning his chin down on top of her head, as if to wrap her totally in his embrace.

"I don't know. I think I had an adrenaline rush going there for a little while, but now that it's all over…" She sighed. "I don't know what I am."

"You never get used to them, Zoey." He unwrapped from the embrace for a moment, to push the stop button. Then he wrapped his arm around her again and simply held her. "And they're always rough, even when the patient pulls through."

"How do you do it, Daniel? How do you put so much time and emotion into a patient, only to end up where we are?"

"It's part of who we are, I suppose. You know—the need to protect and take care of." The way he needed to protect and take care of Zoey in this moment.

Zoey relaxed into his embrace and didn't respond. The elevator didn't move. The call light didn't go off, telling them they needed to proceed to another floor. And, for the very first time, Daniel felt totally at ease with another woman in his arms. No guilt. No memories. Just this moment. This moment that defined so many things he'd been afraid to define.

How it happened, he wasn't sure. But it did happen. He kissed her, and it felt natural, like it was meant to be. And, while it wasn't a kiss of platonic friendship, or even the kiss of a passionate lover, it was a soul-shattering kiss. One that reached him in places he thought were unreachable. A gentle touching of the lips turning quickly into the light probing of their tongues. Hands grabbing hold, clinging. Breaths mingling as one. Dear God, the kiss that he'd feared so much yet wanted so desperately.

Surprisingly, Zoey didn't press to end the kiss, as he'd expected she would do. Rather, she reached up, winding her hands around his neck, and fit her body into the contours of his. And such a nice fit it was. So familiar, and yet so new. "Daniel," she whispered, pulling back slightly. "We shouldn't be doing this."

She was right, of course. They shouldn't be. *He* shouldn't be. And, just like that, Elizabeth came flooding back. "Sorry," he said, dropping his arms to his side, and stepping back. Feeling exhilarated and guilty as hell, all at the same time. "Guess it was a reaction to the moment." A moment that was now over.

Zoey started the elevator up again and turned to face the button panel. "I'm glad you were here to face this with me, Daniel," she said, her voice tainted slightly with a quiver. "And I apologize for getting carried away."

"I think we were both carried away." He didn't step up to stand beside her for the remainder of the ride down to the second floor. Didn't look over to see the smile that had crept to Zoey's face. The contented smile...

"So, do you and Maddie have big plans for the evening?" she asked.

He knew she was trying to sound nonchalant. Avoiding the obvious. Trying to come off as unaffected. Trying to put the kiss out of her mind. That was the way she was, always moving away from things that drew her in emotionally, and he understood that need in her. He didn't like it, but understood it. "Maddie's going to spend the night with her grandmother.

And I'm going home to collapse. Physical exertion, mental exertion…it all combines and makes me tired."

"Then you're not up to dinner tonight?"

Just the two of them? And after the kiss? What a surprise! "Are you asking?"

"Maybe. If you're up to it."

When the elevator came to a stop and the doors opened, they stepped out together, then stopped in the middle of the hallway and turned to face each other. "Are you sure about this, Zoey?" he asked her. "Because I don't want you feeling like you're under some obligation to me because we…"

"Because we gave in to a moment of weakness?"

"Is that what you think it was?"

"What else could it be?"

She knew what it could be. He was sure of that. But he was also sure that she was denying it to herself, and far be it from him to rob her of that delusion. Especially since he expected his own denial to pop up any moment. "It could be the two of us, going back to my place and making omelets."

"Omelets sound good," she said, but tentatively.

Daniel noticed her reaction and wondered if he should have suggested they go to a public place. Somewhere where they could avoid being alone together again. "Or we could go grab Chinese or Italian."

"No. Omelets are fine."

"But you're not sure about coming to my place."

"Maybe, a little."

"Are you hesitant because of Elizabeth?" he asked her. "Because the last time you were there…" *Elizabeth had died.*

"No, I'm fine with that. It's just that this day has been so different, and right now I'm not sure how I feel about anything."

"It was a nice kiss, Zoey."

"But it was more than a kiss between friends. Don't you feel guilty about that?"

"I probably will, once I've had time to think about it. You were my first since Elizabeth."

"And there I am. Coming in behind Elizabeth, again. Another kiss, another *anything*, can't work if I'm always having to stand in line."

She was right, of course. It was his fault she was in this awkward position. But for the life of him he couldn't think how to remedy it, because all remedies took Elizabeth away from him, and he wasn't sure he was ready for that yet. Not even for Zoey. "So I take it you don't want an omelet?"

"I didn't say that," she said.

"Then you *do* want an omelet?"

"I didn't say that, either."

"Do you know what you *do* want, Zoey?"

"If I knew, you'd be the first one I'd tell."

And, if he knew what *he* wanted, Zoey would be the first one *he'd* tell.

# CHAPTER SEVEN

"No, I DON'T WANT hot peppers in my omelet," Zoey stated emphatically, turning up her nose at the suggestion. "Don't care for them."

"Ever?" Daniel asked, smiling as he placed the carton of eggs back in the fridge.

"Ever! Don't like to eat them, don't like to look at them…" She shuddered. "Especially don't like the after-burn that comes with them."

"But I love them. The hotter, the better."

"Then, by all means, put them in your omelet. Just make sure none of them encroach on mine." She wasn't a fanatic about what she liked to eat. Pretty much, she'd eat anything. But she didn't like extra-spicy food, and Daniel's peppers were extra-spicy.

"What about putting a small amount of hot pepper in a recipe? Something like a stew, or maybe nacho cheese?"

"You're testing my limits here, Daniel. I

don't like hot!" She handed him a big, juicy tomato and the knife to cut it with.

"OK, I get the hot thing. Some people just can't take the heat."

"I sweat, and my eyes water. And that's not even to mention how my throat feels."

"But you're sure you like eggs? Because we can fix something else if you don't."

"Eggs aren't spicy, and spicy is the only thing I don't eat."

"But I could put hot sauce in the eggs," he teased.

"And I could go home and fix a tuna-salad sandwich."

"Or stay here with me and trust that I won't go near the peppers and hot sauce tonight, even though they're usually a prominent ingredient in the omelets I fix for myself."

"Eggs, cheese, non-spicy veggies…that's what I want. So, if you can do that without being tempted to betray me, we'll get along fine."

"Is an onion too spicy?"

"Onions are OK."

"And radishes?"

"Radishes in an omelet?" She shook her head. "Sounds peculiar to me."

"Oh, I wasn't going to put a radish in the omelet. I just wanted to see if you like them."

"They make me burp." She recognized the Vidalia onion in the fridge and was glad she found a sweet variety. "So I don't eat them."

"So now, that's hot peppers, hot sauce and radishes. Anything else I should know about you?"

"Is this a food quiz?" she asked as she grabbed a knife from the drawer to dice the onion. "Or are you at a loss for better conversation?"

"Just trying to get to know you."

"Through my eating preferences?"

"Want to talk about your reading preferences instead? Personally, I like biographies. Especially ones that have to do with the Civil War. Oh, and medieval anything."

"I like mysteries, especially the ones that have a little romance included. And I like medical dramas, too."

"I read medical *journals*, and they're pretty dramatic."

Zoey laughed. "Not the same." This was fun, cooking with him, engaging in light, almost nonsensical conversation. It was something that would be so easy to get used to.

"Well, I haven't really read a novel in a couple of years, so I guess that ends our book discussion. Want to move on to music?"

"In a word, classical."

"As in Bach, Beethoven and the rest of the gang?" He scooped onions, tomato and a cut-up zucchini into a bowl and mixed them all together.

"I love the solo piano, so I'm particularly fond of Chopin."

"I don't know about Chopin so much, but I do like Chain."

"Chain?"

"The late, great Harry Chain. Great song-writer. Great singer."

"Then you like the oldies?"

"Oldies—oh, and jazz."

"I like jazz, too."

"Then we'll have to go to a jazz club some night. I know a great place downtown. Used to go there a lot with..." He shook his head. A reminiscent smile touched his lips. "Actually, there's another place near Everett that's supposed to be good. Maybe we'll try *that* some night."

So he didn't want to take her to one of the places where he had fond memories of Elizabeth. They'd already gone to Giovanni's, another place he and Elizabeth had gone to, and she imagined that had been rough on him. So, what else dredged up his memories? Cooking together in the kitchen? Maybe something as simple as omelets?

It occurred to Zoey that there would always be an Elizabeth-shaped stumbling block in the road, and that thought took her completely out of the lighthearted moment they'd been having. Elizabeth—a brilliant cook, a brilliant attorney, a brilliant everything. And here Zoey was, feeling so inadequate. It made her wonder what Daniel saw in her. All this was beginning to make Zoey wish she'd never come here this evening. There was still too much of Elizabeth here. Too many remnants, too many memories. Her presence absolutely filled every nook and cranny of Daniel's house, if not his life, which intimidated Zoey.

*Am I trying to measure up?* Zoey asked herself while Daniel cracked the eggs for the omelet and she grated the cheese. Truthfully, she didn't know. Didn't know why it mattered to her so much. But it did.

"Elizabeth lived a very full life," Zoey said. It was a hard thing to say, as Zoey was beginning to doubt her own capabilities when compared to anything Elizabeth had accomplished.

"You do, too," Daniel stated. He pulled two plates down from the kitchen cabinet and set them next to the stove. "I mean, look at what you do! It's amazing."

Amazing, maybe. But could it hold a candle to Elizabeth? "My life is my work. There's nothing else."

"Because you want it that way?" he asked. Standing at the kitchen counter, ready to put the omelets together and cook them, he turned sideways to study her. "Or because you've never put yourself out there to see what else you can find?"

"I suppose you put *yourself* out there!" she snapped, feeling so inferior right now that all she wanted to do was run away and bury her head in the sand somewhere.

"I'm putting myself out there with you, and I'm sure not getting very far."

He was being so unusually forward it almost hurt her feelings. "You don't know me at all, Daniel."

"Through no fault of my own. I've been trying, Zoey. Every chance I get."

"I know you have, and I appreciate that."

"But I want you to do more than appreciate it."

"What?" she asked him. "What do you want me to do?"

"Relax a little. Sometimes you get so close, then all of a sudden it's like you have second thoughts and you pull back. The thing is, I don't want you to pull back because, in spite of it all, I enjoy being around you. But the problem is, I can't figure you out. Can't figure what you really want. And you don't make it easy for me to find out."

"Why does it mean that much to you?" she asked him.

"Honestly, I don't know. Maybe it's as simple as I don't like being rejected. Or maybe it's more complicated, like I'm developing feelings for you." He shrugged. "Take your pick."

"What if I don't want you to have feelings for me?"

"I don't think that's up to you." He smiled at her. "You can't control everything, Zoey. I know you might want to, but some things simply happen because they happen, and there's nothing about them that you can control."

"Like your feelings for me?" This was getting deep. Too deep. Probably because, in spite of all her efforts to hold back, she was also developing feelings. But with feelings came hopes and dreams, neither of which she could afford to have with Daniel.

"I probably shouldn't have said anything because now you're thinking about running away. Aren't you?"

"Not running away so much as being more cautious." This night wasn't turning out as she'd planned. What she'd wanted was a quiet dinner for two, some pleasant and inconsequential conversation, and a lingering feeling of contentment. What she was getting, however, was the feeling that she wanted more than she could even admit to herself.

"Because I challenge you?"

"Not you, Daniel. It's everything you come with that challenges me. And I didn't come here to be challenged. I mean, you're obviously looking for something I am not, which leaves us…"

"Grappling with what to do," he supplied.

"See, I could understand if this was just about sex. It's been a while for you, a while for me, so we could do it—sweat out a few good moments together, then get on with it. Or if this was about simply wanting a new friend we could commit to that, even with all these uneasy feelings I think we're both having about where we stand with each other, and move forward from there. But you're right. It's more complicated than that, and I don't think either of us is prepared to deal with that."

"Why do we have to be prepared for anything? Can't we just take it as it comes?"

"No, because I have to see where I'm going, and I don't want to be forced into anything that I can't see. My past history proves that I didn't used to do that, and I don't want to repeat the past." Marriage to Brad had taught her a very hard lesson. With him, taking it as it came meant she'd jumped in with her whole heart only to be kicked around for it. Next time she would prepare herself for it before she jumped in with anything. Use her head first. Not her heart. And, in Daniel's case, her head was screaming a succession of "be carefuls" at her. Unfortunately, her heart was also screaming, and it wasn't a warning to beware.

"Do you think I'm trying to force you into something, Zoey?"

"I don't know. Are you?"

"That day in the coffee shop, I was glad to see you. The next time I saw you, at the fundraising banquet, I wondered if we could be friends, and I suppose I acted on that. But I'm not trying to force you into being my friend, lover, partner or anything else if you don't want to be."

At this point, Zoey wasn't sure what she wanted. "The thing is, after Elizabeth's death we went a whole year without ever seeing each other, then suddenly we're involved. And I don't know where that's going. I can't see past right now!"

"Maybe because I'm always treading on eggshells when I'm around you, trying not to frighten you. And I'm not even sure what it is about me that frightens you."

"Your own eggshells, Daniel. That's what frightens me."

"My eggshells?"

"Your attachment to Elizabeth. It's not a bad thing. In fact, I think it's a very good thing. But it consumes so much of you, I wonder if there's any room left in you for something else." *Or someone else.*

"I'm painfully aware of that, Zoey. And I'm trying hard to step away from it, but at the end of the day I'm still a widower who hasn't found his direction yet. And it's not that I don't want to, because I do."

"Which leaves us where?" she asked him, suddenly exhausted from all the talk. They were going around in circles now, pointing out all the pitfalls but not able to get around them.

Daniel sighed as he scooped the prepared omelets onto the plates and headed toward the kitchen table—a casual set-up across from the kitchen sink. "It leaves us forging a friendship that shouldn't be this difficult. It also leaves us wondering if we're building up to something more than just a friendship."

Zoey shook her head. "Well, I guess we both have a lot of obstacles, don't we?"

"Moving forward's tough, Zoey. God knows I'm trying, but it's something I never counted on having to do alone."

"And it's something I never counted on doing with anybody."

Daniel chuckled. "Aren't we the pair?" He pulled out a chair for Zoey and, once she had taken a seat, he sat down opposite her. "I think I've always had a problem with moving forward. Basically, I can be a very contented man, happy with what I have, happy with where I am. Contentment comes easily to me and I don't like to test it."

"Were you always like that, even when you were a kid?" she asked him. "Or did Elizabeth bring about that contentment?"

"A little bit of both, I think. When I was a kid I always held back, and that was fine by me. Damien took the lead, and as often as not I lagged behind and watched, not sure what I could do to keep up with him. But that was OK for me because I was always good where I was. And with Elizabeth..." He sighed and his eyes glowed with a distant memory. "I can't even begin to describe how it was with her. She had this amazing way of making me happy, even with the little things that other people probably wouldn't notice."

"Such as?"

"We went out and bought juice glasses one time. They had sunflowers on them—pretty, I suppose, but they really weren't of much consequence. Elizabeth liked them, though. She smiled every time she picked one up and saw the sunflower. And, for some strange reason, I looked forward to that moment in our morning routine. It was one of those little things…"

Zoey imagined he still had those sunflowers. "My husband never noticed anything about me except my paychecks."

"That's too bad, because there are a lot of things to notice."

"Are you trying to flatter me?"

Daniel shook his head, smiling. "Just being honest."

"Well, your honesty stirs a lack of confidence in me."

"Seriously?"

"Seriously," she admitted, taking a first bite of her omelet, even though her appetite had disappeared a while ago. "Everybody lies, Daniel, when they're trying to get something."

"So what do you think I'm trying to get?"

Zoey shrugged. "I haven't figured that out yet."

"But you're hanging around to find out?"

"Maybe I am." In spite of her misgivings about him, he stimulated her in ways no one else had ever done. His directness caused her to think. "Time will tell, I suppose."

"Do you realize that you're implying we've got more time together?"

"Isn't that what you want?" she asked him.

"I think the more appropriate question here is, isn't that what *you* want?"

"You're twisting my words." As well as her heart. Daniel was a man who could be so easy to love. So did she, on some unconscious level, want that?

The conversation eventually turned to Maddie, then to Zoey's hobby of climbing and her fascination with keeping fit, and eventually to Daniel's twin who was, apparently, getting tangled up in a complicated relationship situation of his own. Nowhere in the conversation, though, was there a mention of their own feelings, doubts and fears. Which was nice, as Zoey didn't want to take all that home with her then try to sleep on it. "The omelet was wonderful," she said, once she'd eaten all she could.

"Next time I'll stop at the store and buy some better ingredients for it. More veggies, better cheese…" He smiled. "A nice bottle of wine, because I like the idea of having wine with an intimate dinner."

She opened her eyes wide and smiled. "You're a romantic." Was it by nature, she wondered, or had it been taught by Elizabeth? An image of Daniel and Elizabeth enjoying an intimate dinner suddenly popped into her mind, but before it could etch itself there indelibly she blinked it away and forced herself to concentrate on the half-eaten omelet on her plate.

"I used to be. I'm sort of out of practice now."

"I've heard it's like riding a bicycle," she said without enthusiasm, as Elizabeth kept trying to force her way back in. "Once you learn, you never really forget."

"Until you fall off the damned thing and skin your knee."

She looked back up at Daniel. "But you're a doctor. You know how to treat a skinned knee." Or an intimate dinner meant for one person but with someone else in mind. "Look, it's getting late, we're both tired and I've got an early appointment in the morning. So I'd better take off."

Daniel pushed back his chair and stood up. "Do you think we could do this again sometime?"

"I'll think about it," she said cautiously.

His eyes sparkled. "Why did I know that's what you'd say?"

"Because I'm predictable?"

"Trust me. You're not predictable, Zoey. Not predictable at all."

Up out of her chair and heading to the front door, Zoey stopped in the middle of Daniel's living room and turned around to face him. He was so dangerously close to her now, she could smell his aftershave, and for an instant she closed her eyes and imagined this to be an intimate moment between them. Like the one they'd had in the elevator earlier. He was taking her into his arms; she was offering herself up to him. Lips meeting. Sighs escaping. It was a wonderful fantasy for that instant, but she put it away so quickly it nearly caused her head to swim.

She did want Daniel, but it was not in a way she could fathom that he wanted to be wanted. Daniel wasn't ready, and maybe he didn't even know that. But she did. Keenly. "Let's talk again in a couple of days," she finally said. "OK?"

"This is where I should jump on that and ask you out on a date. But I won't. Instead, I'll just wait for you to call."

"Promise?"

He leaned forward and brushed a light kiss on her lips. One of those platonic friendship kisses. "Promise." Then he showed her to the door and waited until she was out of sight before he closed it.

She could hear the click behind her. Could almost see Daniel still standing by the door, wondering what he'd just done.

What *had* they just done? she wondered as she got in her car and drove away.

He'd been pacing the floor for an hour now. Restless, perturbed. Guilty as hell. What had come over him, anyway? He'd taken on Zoey like he had a right. Which he didn't. The plain truth was, the lady had a hard time even admitting to a friendship, and here he was pushing toward more. And feeling rotten and disloyal about it, to boot.

"OK," he said to the mirror in his hall. "You're not married. So why turn one little kiss in the elevator into such a big deal?"

*Because I'm an idiot,* he thought to himself. Zoey hadn't been throwing out any signals other than one that pointed to a mild friendship. And here he'd gone all presumptuous on her and gone so far as to stop the elevator and kiss her like it would be his last kiss for all time. *Idiot!*

"Damn," he said, wanting to throw a towel over the mirror to block the image that looked back at him. He hardly knew that man anymore. He wasn't sure he wanted to know him, yet wasn't sure he was ready to let him go. "So what happens next?" he asked, as if his mirror image would answer him.

Should he pursue Zoey, with the clear understanding that she was as likely to turn her back on him as she was to welcome him?

Daniel walked into his bedroom and stopped at the bureau, where he looked at one of Elizabeth's last pictures. It was sitting on top, with nothing to obstruct it. That picture was the last thing he saw every night, before he went to sleep, and it was also the first thing he saw every morning. It had been taken in a happy moment, before her diagnosis, and it was a true testament to a beautiful life. A beautiful life…the life he wanted back. Or wanted to forge again, in a different direction.

"God help me, I want more than a casual relationship with her, Elizabeth," he said to the image. "And I don't know what to do about it."

Elizabeth wouldn't have wanted him so confused. He knew that beyond a shadow of a doubt. Which meant he was the one holding himself back. Sure, he'd been a little forward with Zoey tonight. Not physically, but in conversation. He'd pushed boundaries, been blunt. And, frankly, it had surprised him, as he still wasn't reconciled to the fact that he was trying to give Zoey a gentle nudge in his direction. Maybe it was loneliness biting at him, causing him to step out of his comfort zone. Or maybe somewhere deep in his subconscious something was telling him that Zoey could be more than simply casual to him. Either way, it confused him.

Daniel twisted his wedding ring, then studied it hard for a moment. Yes, all these strange feelings did confuse him, as he didn't know where to put them. Maybe in time he would. Or maybe in time he'd finally reconcile himself to the idea that he'd already had the best and, from there, there was no place else to go.

Zoey's day started in a blur. She felt hungover, even though she hadn't had a drop to drink the night before. "I'm fine," she told Sally, on her way to her desk. "And if you think I look like hell, don't ask why, because I don't have an answer for you."

"I wasn't going to say you look like hell. More like, you look…unlike you."

"It's a headache. Nothing big."

"You've got bags under your eyes."

Zoey went for the compact mirror in her purse and took a look. Sally was right. She did have bags. "I didn't get much sleep."

"Are you in love?" Sally asked. "Baggy eyes from lost sleep are often a symptom."

Love? That wasn't something she took lightly. Especially since all her restlessness was tied up in Daniel. "I'm just overworked. I need a vacation."

"You need a life," Sally admonished her. "A real life, outside your nursing duties."

"Like I've got time for anything else." Zoey poured herself a cup of coffee from the communal office pot and, instead of heading for her own desk, sat down across the desk from Sally. While she wasn't about to confide in Sally, it was nice to have someone to talk to. "It's just that, sometimes I get wrapped up in things that aren't in my best interests." That might be Daniel.

"Oh, right. That doctor. How's that working out for you, by the way?"

"There's nothing to work out. We're just… friends."

"Famous last words."

"Look, I don't have time to get involved. OK? And, even if I did, Daniel wouldn't be the one. He's too preoccupied with other things in his life to take on something else."

"Maybe you should find a way to become one of those things he's preoccupied with."

"Right. Like it's just that simple."

Sally laughed. "Trust me. In matters of the heart, nothing is ever simple."

"Tell me about it." Zoey picked up her mug and went to her office. There was enough paperwork there to keep her busy for a couple of days. Enough paperwork to keep her distracted from the kiss. The kiss…now, what was that about?

"The order specifically calls for an anti-fungal cream, *not* a hydrocortisone cream." It wasn't a huge mistake; no harm done. But he was peeved. Peeved at everything today, it seemed. "Read the chart again and get the order right this time."

"Sorry, Doctor," the nurse said, backing away from him. "I'll get it ordered right away."

Daniel nodded, drawing in a long, slow breath. It calmed him for the moment, and he smiled at the poor nurse who'd just taken the brunt of his bad mood. "Sorry I snapped," he said, offering no explanation, like he was having a bad day or the world simply irritated him right now.

"It was my mistake," she admitted.

"We all make mistakes," he conceded, then walked away from the nurses' station. He knew why he was in a bad mood, and he'd thought about calling Zoey to see if he could remedy it. But, every time he picked up his cell phone to make that call, he'd had second thoughts. Second thoughts that he carried with him even now, well into the afternoon.

"I understand you're not having a good day," Walter Downing said as he joined up with Daniel in the hall.

"Word spreads fast, doesn't it?"

"We're not that big of a hospital, Daniel. And people here are concerned about you."

"But I'm doing fine."

"Are you really? Because I sure as hell don't see it."

"It shows that much?"

"I've heard rumors."

"Not rumors," Daniel admitted. "Truths, depending on whether you're talking about my personal life or my professional one."

"Anything I can do to help you, either personally or professionally? I've had a little bit of experience with both, you know."

Walter was a kind man, and he'd been a godsend during Elizabeth's illness, allowing Daniel off work any time he needed. But Daniel didn't consider him friend enough for a confidence, so he simply crammed his hands into his pockets and continued on toward his office. "I'll do better," he promised Walter, who continued to keep up with him down the hall. "And I appreciate the concern."

"You know I'm retiring in a year, and you're in line to replace me."

Daniel did know that. And he was pleased that his name was being considered. He'd worked hard to get to where he was, and it was his every intention to keep moving forward in his career. Unlike his personal life. "You'll be missed," Daniel told the older man.

"And you'll be welcomed in my position, but you've got to take better control of things, Daniel. You've got to make more of an effort to keep your life balanced, because if and when you do get the position being able to keep everything in its proper place will be key to your ability to do everything you need to accomplish...both personally and professionally."

"Is this with reference to the banquet I didn't want to attend?" For a perfectly good reason. Although now, he was glad Walter had insisted he attend.

"That, and other things. I know you're overwhelmed right now, especially bouncing back and forth between being a doctor and a single dad, and I understand it's a struggle. I sympathize with you for that. But you're going to have to get hold of yourself at some point."

"You mean my social life?" Did his lack of one show that drastically?

"I mean your life all around. You've been through a tragedy, and I can't even pretend to understand how you're carrying on afterward, but that was a year ago, and since then you've seemed to shut so many things out."

"But I do my job," Daniel protested, stopping short of his office door.

"And you do it well. No complaints there."

"Then what's the complaint?"

"The way you treat yourself. You keep pushing yourself, Daniel, but I'm not sure that it's in the best direction."

"I only have one direction."

"Which could be the problem."

Walter was right about this. Heading in only one direction was a problem, but he didn't know how to go any other way. Even Zoey wasn't the solution, although he was treating her like she was. No, the solution was within himself, buried so deep he couldn't see it. Or didn't want to see it. "I'm doing the best I can, Walter. If my work is suffering, let me know, because I love what I do here and I don't want to do anything to mess it up. But if you're concerned about my social life, well, there's not much I can do about it. I'm already committed as much as I can commit, and there's nothing

I can do to make my situation any different than it is."

"Just be good to yourself, Daniel. Once you can do that, I think everything else will fall into place."

Be good to himself. Nice words. But they were so far off, Daniel couldn't even begin to think how to apply them. Sure, he pushed himself forward with Zoey, but that wasn't about being good to himself. It was more about trying to see what he was capable of doing. And so far, with Zoey, he was failing miserably. Probably his fault. No—*definitely* his fault.

Sighing, Daniel walked on into his office and slumped down in his chair. It was time to take stock of his life. He'd known that for a while, and Zoey was only emphasizing the reality of it. *Why couldn't life have been simpler?* he asked himself as he twisted his wedding ring. It was a habit he'd taken up months ago when Elizabeth was filling his thoughts. Only now, his wedding ring represented something else. Something that was holding him back.

He slipped it off for a moment and studied his naked hand. It looked…wrong. And it felt so empty, like a great hole in his soul opened up when the ring came off. So he put it back on, leaned back in his chair and closed his eyes. What the hell was he going to do?

# CHAPTER EIGHT

IT HAD BEEN a restless three days since she'd last seen Daniel, and Zoey couldn't count the number of times she'd considered calling him. Of course, she hadn't gone through with it, or else she wouldn't be thinking about it right now. Also, she'd caught herself hanging around her office more often these past few days, making excuses to be there when, in the past, she'd tried hard to stay away. She'd done her fair share of staring out the window, too, hoping she'd catch a glimpse of him coming or going. Without binoculars, though, she really hadn't been able to discern one person from another.

So Zoey was caught up in this fantasy world that was playing out in ways she couldn't control. Or maybe didn't want to control. What of it? She was entitled to a little daydreaming every now and then, wasn't she? Entitled to think thoughts that had never before crossed her mind. Yes, she was, as long as it didn't get out of hand. Still, it was a concern that the object of her daydreams was exclusively Daniel. Mountains, rivers or ocean shores would have been a better choice for her rambling thoughts, but every time she let her mind wander it went straight to him. No detours, no hesitation. Sometimes he was so prevalent it seemed like he was popping in and out at will.

Zoey glanced out the window for at least the twentieth time since she'd arrived at her office an hour ago, then looked back down at her desk. It was covered with cost estimations for the upcoming quarter, something that bored her to tears when she was required to tackle the budget. Try as she might, she couldn't focus on it. All those numbers were spinning circles in her brain, going nowhere but round and round.

"Shoot!" she said aloud, shoving the stack of papers aside. There was no use pretending she was going to do any good here. She wasn't. Not today. Not when she was so restless. And most especially not when her mind was drifting again, only this time not drifting to what had already happened between them but, rather, to what might be in their future. That was, if they had some kind of a future together. Something more than what they had now. "Get it together," she cautioned herself as she pushed back from her desk, preparing to leave. "You're letting it get away from you."

Getting away from her? That was an understatement, if ever there was one. Thoughts of Daniel were consuming her, eating up every spare inch of her brain. Creeping in and holding on. "So quit thinking about him," she chided herself, her eyes still glued to the window next to her desk. "And quit talking to yourself! People are going to think you're crazy." Of course, *she* was beginning to think she was crazy. But, crazy or not, her advice to herself was falling on deaf ears as she wanted to see Daniel. Desperately.

"I've got an appointment," she told Sally a few minutes later, once she'd reconciled herself to the fact that she was wasting time being here in the office.

"Are you going out in the field again? I thought one of the other nurses was covering for you this afternoon while you got some of the paperwork done." Sally tilted her head downward and looked at Zoey over the rims of her white-framed glasses. "Or aren't you going back to work in the field?"

"I am being covered adequately, so that's not a problem. And the truth of the matter is,

I don't want to be cooped up here today, so I'm going out."

"Since you don't want to be here, where, exactly, do you want to be?" A twinkle came to Sally's eyes. "Does he wear a stethoscope around his neck and is he handsome?"

"He's a patient," she said, trying to overcome her agitation. "He dismissed us and I want to go talk to him about that."

"And possibly run into your doctor?"

"Daniel's not my doctor. And the hospital's a big place. There's no guaranteeing that I'll just run into him."

"You would if you called him to tell him you're on your way over." Sally pushed her glasses back up her nose. "Seriously, Zoey. If you're interested in the man, make it a point to run into him, because I don't want all this grumpiness coming into my office every day."

"I'm not grumpy," Zoey argued. But she was, and she knew it.

"Tell that to somebody who doesn't know you—which is *not* me. Anyway, are you coming back later on?" Sally asked her.

"Depends," she said.

"On what?"

"On whether or not I bump into someone who makes me a better offer." Zoey smiled at the prospect, even though she really didn't hold out a lot of hope that Daniel would ask anything if their paths crossed. She'd been too aloof their last time together. Too cautious. Too mistrusting.

Zoey gave her friend a farewell wave and headed out the office door. Thoughts of prospects and let-downs carried with her all the way over to the hospital and all the way up to the intensive care unit where the nursing staff was preparing to transfer Mr. Baumgartner. Since the staff was a good ten minutes out from releasing him from the unit, Zoey decided to wander on down to the room where they were taking him and wait there. On her way though, she caught sight of Daniel walking down the hall, coming directly toward her. He was leading a group of medical students, all with brand-new stethoscopes hanging around their necks, totally caught up in explaining something that was holding their rapt attention. In his element, Daniel was quite something. Magnificent, actually. A stunner of a man. Also a stunner of a doctor, judging by the way his students were practically mesmerized by his every word.

Zoey didn't want to be caught staring at him, and she didn't want to distract him, either, so she stepped out of the way, semi-concealing herself up against the wall and behind a rolling blood-pressure monitor. From that vantage point she observed Daniel for a moment, suddenly feeling a swell of pride over his accomplishments. They were vast, she knew. Elizabeth had been so proud of his value as a doctor, and she'd said she was the one who had to point out that worth, as Daniel was too humble a man to do it for himself.

Now, as Zoey watched on, she could see how right Elizabeth had been, and she didn't have to look past the admiring expressions on his students' faces, as they were clearly a true testament to how good he was.

She'd seen other attending doctors lecturing other medical students before, as it was a common sight in a teaching hospital, and none of that had ever impressed her much. Staff members got used to it, didn't pay any attention to it, except occasionally when the exuberance of the students got in the way of nurses and other medical personnel trying to do their jobs. Yet seeing Daniel leading his group of students… She'd never really imagined him in this position, and this different side of him fascinated her. In fact, it fascinated her so much that her first impulse was to blend herself into his group, when they walked by her, just to listen to him teach. But she'd stand out, owing to the fact that she was dressed in her usual navy-blue scrubs and the students were in street clothes covered by short, white doctors' jackets.

Well, it was a nice idea, but not a practical one, so Zoey's second choice was to find an escape route that would take her down another hall before Daniel set eyes on her.

"Zoey?" she heard him call out as she was scurrying away.

So much for not getting caught. "Hello, Dr. Caldwell," she said as she turned slowly to face him, noting that his medical students were closing in all around him.

"Is there something I can do for you?" he asked. A slight smile touched his lips—one so slight that his students wouldn't have noticed it.

But Zoey noticed it—the smile, the dimples popping out, the crinkles around his smiling eyes. She swallowed hard and smiled back at him. "I'm here to see Mr. Baumgartner. I heard he was being released from the ICU today, so I thought I'd see if he had a change of heart about home nursing care…whenever you're ready to release him again."

"He's pretty distressed right now," Daniel cautioned. "And embarrassed, I think."

She felt bad for the man. In a moment of weakness, Mr. Baumgartner had tried to do something stupid, and now he was faced with having to deal with his actions. "Is he doing OK physically, though?" That was her main concern for him.

"As well as can be expected. I had a couple of my medical students sit with him for a while this morning, and he insisted to them that he wanted to go home as soon as possible."

Zoey pursed her lips and blew out a contemplative breath. "That's a tough one, isn't it?"

"Considering that we have no right to keep him here against his will—unless we admit him to the psychiatric ward for a seventy-two-hour observation, which I don't want to do—I guess you'd say it is."

"But couldn't you put him on a psychiatric hold for his own good, since he did try to kill himself?"

"I could, but that would only make him angrier than he already is. And I'm afraid that anger could take a toll on his health. So I'd rather try to keep him in a regular room for as long as I can and watch him from there."

"You're still hoping for an optimistic outcome with him, aren't you?"

Daniel shrugged. "It's what I hope for with all my patients."

"But Mr. Baumgartner is more at risk than most of your patients." She looked around at the med students, many of whom were actually taking notes of this conversation.

"Well, I did tell him that if he has any hope of going home in the near future, and resuming his life as best he can, he'd have to cooperate with our plan for him. He grumbled about it, of course. But I think I got through to him."

She was confident Daniel had gotten through to him. In his understated way, Daniel had the ability to get through to anybody he wanted to. After all, he'd gotten through to her, and she'd fought him on it. "Well, I'm going to go see him anyway. Maybe talk him into letting me follow him again once he's out of here. I *can* tell him that's part of your plan for him, can't I?"

Daniel turned to his students. "Miss Evans is the hospice nurse who was caring for our patient before he tried to commit suicide."

All the students scribbled that little piece of information into their notes.

"Yes, do tell him," Daniel directed at Zoey. "Now, give me fifteen minutes to finish up with my students, and by then Mr. Baumgartner should be settled into his room. We can go see him together."

She wasn't in a position to turn Daniel down, because after all he *was* Mr. Baumgartner's doctor. So she sucked it in and smiled.

"I'll be down at the nurses' station, reading his chart." With that she walked away from him, knowing full well that he was watching her. It was hard keeping a proper gait under the circumstances and she was grateful that she had to veer off down one more hall to get to where she was going, as Daniel's intense scrutiny caused goosebumps to run up and down her arms, caused her knees to go weak and caused her heart to flutter. And she was grateful for the wall that held her up once she turned the corner and slumped against it.

The departure of his medical students couldn't have come fast enough, once Daniel had agreed to meet Zoey in Mr. Baumgartner's room. It wasn't that he wanted to be rid of them, as he enjoyed the teaching aspects of his job. He'd been the young, eager med student once, and his own mentor had been largely responsible for the kind of doctor he was today. Still, Daniel wanted to see Zoey. Under any pretense. It had been three days. Three days of memories of a simple kiss. Three days of admonishing himself for doing it and congratulating himself, all at the same time.

"I'm back," he said to his patient as he entered the room. Zoey was already there, seated on a chair next to Mr. Baumgartner's bed.

"Not again," Mr. Baumgartner groaned. "I thought I'd gotten rid of you the first time."

"For the moment, maybe. But I'm still your doctor."

"Unfortunately," the man growled.

"You know you like me," Daniel said, smiling.

"I used to like you until you started bothering me."

"For your own good, Mr. Baumgartner. That's all I'm here for...your own good."

"Well, you're not going to change my mind, young man," Mr. Baumgartner warned him. "She's not, either." He pointed to Zoey. "I'm going home when I feel better, and nobody's going to stop me."

"I'll dismiss you when you're up to it," Daniel said quite evenly.

"I don't care if you dismiss me, or if I dismiss myself. Either way, I'm going home," the man insisted.

"With home nursing care?" Zoey asked. "Like before?"

"You're a damn hospice nurse, and I don't want the likes of you doing anything for me. It's a reminder of the things I can't do for myself any longer," Mr. Baumgartner said angrily.

"But you may regain some of your abilities," Zoey said, trying to sound hopeful about it.

"Not with people waiting on me hand and foot, I won't. Especially people who are waiting for me to get worse...or die!"

"We're only trying to help you, Mr. Baumgartner. That's all. And it's not my intention to make you feel bad, because you do need that help now." Zoey turned to Daniel. "Maybe we could back off the frequency of our visits a little bit so Mr. Baumgartner won't feel so inundated."

Daniel looked at Mr. Baumgartner. "But there's still the concern over what you might try to do to yourself again."

"It was a moment of weakness," Mr. Baumgartner said. "I won't try it again."

"I didn't think you'd try it in the first place," Daniel stated.

"Like I said, it was a moment of weakness. But I'm not usually a weak person, doc. It's just that it all caught up with me, and I didn't know how to face waiting around until the bitter end."

Baumgartner was winding down, giving in; Zoey could see that in him and she felt sorry for the man. He was angry and scared. He didn't know which way to turn anymore. And he resented the condition he was in. "We're just concerned for you," she told her former patient. "That's why we're here now. That's why we're trying to reason with you."

"Like I said," Mr. Baumgartner said, "It won't happen again."

Daniel nodded. "I understand, but that still doesn't change what happened already, and that's all I have to go on."

"So I'll get that damned psychiatric counseling you suggested this morning. As long as you don't lock me up in their ward. Will that convince you that I *can* go home?"

"First off, I'm not locking you up anywhere. You don't need that kind of intense observation. I hope you don't prove me wrong on that, because if you do…" He shook his head. "I don't even want to think about what I'll have to do to protect you for your own good. And, second, the psychiatric consult is a good start. But you've still got a long way to go before I'm convinced that you can leave here."

Mr. Baumgartner dropped back onto his pillow and shut his eyes. "I guess I really messed things up, didn't I?"

"We all make mistakes," Zoey said, reaching across to pat his hand. "Some of us more so than others."

The interaction between Zoey and Mr. Baumgartner was good, and Daniel was confident that when he released the man this time he'd allow Zoey to come back and take care of him. He hoped so anyway, because he still held out some hope that his patient's time wouldn't be counted by days or weeks, but rather by months or even years. The last test results and X-rays he'd looked at earlier today *had* showed some marginal improvement.

"He's a tough old guy," Daniel said to Zoey a little while later.

"And stubborn," she added. "Hopefully not too stubborn that he refuses medical help once he's out of here."

"Time will tell, I suppose." Daniel walked Zoey to the elevator, but paused before he pushed the button. "Care for a cup of coffee? Or lunch, if you haven't eaten yet?"

"You always ask, don't you?"

"And you always refuse. But one of these days…" He smiled as his finger pressed the down button.

"Maybe today. But only because I haven't eaten and I'm hungry."

"Really?" That was a surprise. After their last evening together, he wouldn't have bet a nickel that she'd do anything with him again. But here she was, on the verge of accepting an invitation. Progress, he thought. Toward what, he wasn't sure. But it was progress nonetheless. "I've got some time right now, if you're serious about it."

"Are you sure? Because I don't want you to get behind with anything."

"I've got med students and residents covering my patients right now, and I'm not due back on the floor for another hour, so I'm good. How about you? This isn't going to eat into your schedule, is it?"

"I had a ton of paperwork to do today, so I've got somebody else covering for me with my patients."

"And the paperwork is done?" he asked.

"As much as I care to get done. What's left over can wait." Or be thrown away, as far as she was concerned.

"I take it you don't like paperwork."

"I like patient care. The rest of it's a necessary evil."

Daniel smiled. "Well, I'm glad you can put your necessary evil aside for a while and turn this into my lucky day." On the elevator, he pushed the number three, which would stop at the cafeteria.

"I think you should hold off on thinking you're lucky until after we go to the cafeteria." Zoey leaned up against the lift wall for the short ride and looked straight ahead, *not* at Daniel. "Things may not turn out as you've planned."

"Does that mean we're going to fight?"

"Nope. I don't want to fight. I don't even want to engage in a deep conversation. Instead, I'd like to keep it light. Talk about the weather, or Maddie, or the thirteen-K run the hospital's going to hold to benefit the pediatric wing."

The elevator stopped and they both got off together, almost shoulder to shoulder. "You running in it?" he asked.

"I don't run," she said, following Daniel through the cafeteria doors and on up to the serving line. She grabbed a tray and pushed it on down the line, picking up the first salad she came to. "But, as you know, I do go to an indoor fitness center and climb a rock wall every now and then. And I have a treadmill at home that I use at least three times a week. Oh, and I power walk."

Coming up behind her, Daniel opted for a plate of poached salmon and couscous along with a bowl of broccoli. "Well, you've got me beat. I was thinking about entering the thirteen-K, but I'm so out of shape now I'm afraid even one K would be a challenge for me."

"You used to work out?" She stopped mid-serving-line and turned back to face him. "I never pictured you as someone who does that."

"Back before Elizabeth got sick, I worked out religiously. Then I got out of the habit, and it's hard getting back in. Especially since all my former exercise time is now devoted to Maddie." He pulled out his wallet and paid the bill, then followed Zoey to the nearest available table.

"I walk in the mornings before work. Every day that I can. Power walking is good for you. Nice cardiovascular workout. You ought to try it sometime."

"Is that an offer?" he asked.

She looked surprised for a second, but her face eventually gave way to compliance. "I suppose, if you want to walk, it is."

"How far do you usually go?" he asked, excited by the prospect of doing something with Zoey on a regular basis.

"About five miles, give or take. I'd do more if I could, but I don't have the time."

"Every day?"

She shook her head. "Right now I'm doing good to get in every other day. But I hope to increase that eventually."

"So what time would I have to get up and get myself going in order to walk with you?" His first thought was about Maddie. Would

Abby agree to take her a couple of hours early on the mornings he walked with Zoey? He hoped so, as any excuse to have time with Maddie was good for Abby.

"It's early, Daniel, because I have to get to work early."

Now she was having second thoughts, trying to warn him off it. He'd caught on to that but he was choosing to ignore it. "How early?"

"Probably about five, since I go out at six. Unless it takes you a long time to shower and get moving."

Ten minutes to shower, ten minutes to dress, ten minutes to grab something to eat, thirty minutes to get Maddie up and over to her grandmother's house—that was his everyday morning already, and this would only make it an hour earlier. Not a problem, he hoped, recalling the time he'd joined up with a group of doctors from the hospital who did an early walk every morning. That hadn't worked out for him as he really did hate early hours. But having those early hours with Zoey…it didn't seem all that bad. "How far from me do you live?"

"About a mile."

That surprised him. Somehow, he'd pictured Zoey living on the other side of Seattle. Maybe a two-hour drive from his house, depending on interstate conditions. But no, she lived in his neighborhood. So close, he was surprised that he hadn't casually bumped into her somewhere. "Since we're so close to each other, I can definitely be at your place by six," he said.

"Then it sounds like we've got a date." Said with obvious reluctance.

He noticed that reluctance and, for a second, thought about backing out. But, damn it, he wanted to be selfish about this. Wanted Zoey all to himself for that occasional hour. "Will that give me enough time to get to the hospital by seven?"

"I power walk, Daniel," she warned him. "Five miles go by fast, and I'm not slowing down for you."

Somehow, he didn't think she would.

"Oh, and if walking isn't enough for you, maybe I'll take you wall-climbing sometime. You're not afraid of heights, are you?"

Not actual physical heights, he wasn't. But this was turning into an emotional height that scared the living daylights out of him.

Zoey tied her walking shoes then wandered over to the window to see if Daniel was approaching yet. She glanced at the clock on her living room wall. Five till six. "Five more minutes, Daniel," she said. "Then I'm leaving here without you."

There was no leeway in her schedule. None whatsoever. And if Daniel didn't catch on to that she had no choice but to leave him behind. That, after tossing and turning in bed last night in anticipation of their walk together this morning.

One more glance out and she still didn't see him so, sighing, she headed to the front door and opened it. Maybe another time, she thought as she stepped out onto her front porch and took a long look up and down her quaint little tree-lined street.

"Looking for me?" he asked, winding a path in from the side of her house.

"Where'd you come from?" she asked him.

He pointed to his car parked down the street. "Been here for ten minutes, waiting for you to come out. Pulled some weeds from your flower garden in the meantime."

"You weeded my garden?" She didn't know what to say to that. It was a nice gesture, but it was also very…familiar. Too familiar, maybe.

"It needed it."

"But I would have done it when I had time."

"Now you don't have to!"

He was awfully chipper for this time of the morning. Somehow, she'd expected him to be sleepy or subdued. Maybe even a little grouchy. But no, Daniel was sunny. She liked it, but she also wondered if this was an everyday occurrence or something he was putting on specifically for her. "Well, if you show up early day after tomorrow, I'll leave some ironing out for you."

Daniel chuckled as he took his place by her side and imitated her in a routine of stretching exercises. First the ankles, then the legs, then the back and finally the shoulders. "How about I send my housekeeper over to do that?"

"You have a housekeeper?" she asked him as she straightened up and prepared to start walking.

"Three times a week. Mondays, Wednesdays and Fridays."

"Oh, ye of the privileged class," Zoey said, keeping a straight face.

"Not privileged so much as needy. I don't have time to take care of my house so I *need* to hire someone to do it for me."

"I hate house-cleaning, but I do it because I don't want somebody else coming in and poking around my things."

"Like your flower bed?" he asked, adjusting his walking pace to hers.

So far they were on a moderate walk, not leisurely, but not too fast. Only for a few moments, though, because once they rounded the first corner Zoey launched into her power walking with a vengeance, leaving Daniel behind. It took him several seconds to catch up to her, and that was when she noticed that he was holding up his end of the walk quite admirably for someone who'd probably never been power walking before. It could be he wasn't so out of shape after all.

She glanced down at his legs. Tan. Nice. Well-muscled. Thank heavens for athletic shorts as they gave her a good view of his lower body. She took a nice, appreciative look "I'm not particular about my flower bed one way or another. In fact, it's a leftover from a couple years ago, when I actually took the time to plant a few things. The house was new to me then, and I was a little more enthusiastic about outside chores and perennial plants."

"But not anymore?" he asked, finding his stride nicely next to her.

"I mow the yard when it needs it. Prune my shrubs when I get around to it. Pull weeds when I have to."

"So what you're telling me is that you lost your enthusiasm?"

"What I'm telling you is that I'm not domestic, and I probably should have bought a condo, where much of the maintenance is done by the condo association, rather than investing in a house."

"It's never too late," he said.

"Maybe it's not, but I'm settled now, and I'm not really good at making major changes in my life."

"Tell me about it," he said, almost under his breath.

Taking her eyes off the course ahead of them, Zoey glanced over at Daniel. "What's that supposed to mean?"

"As Dylan Thomas might have said, you don't go gentle into that good night."

"That's referring to death."

"Maybe so, but I'm paraphrasing it into meaning your life."

"OK, so I find it hard to make changes. Big deal. We're all allowed to have our *foibles*, aren't we?" She wasn't angry, but she was put off by his keen observation of her. Honestly, she hadn't known he was looking that closely. Why was he? she wondered as they rounded yet another corner and headed in the direction of a neighborhood park.

# CHAPTER NINE

OVERALL, ZOEY WAS generally pleased with the way her walk with Daniel went. They hadn't chatted too much, as it distracted them from what they were doing. Zoey was fine with that, however, as the quietness between them gave her more time to think about how much she enjoyed his company. Daniel was an interesting man and it was easy to see why Elizabeth had fallen for him. In a subtle kind of a way, he was someone who truly didn't know his effect on people. Humble. Smart.

He had an interesting face, too, and she'd had the chance to study it along their route, catching sideways glances of him every now and then. The way he concentrated—with a slight frown and a firmly set mouth—was downright irresistible, as far as Zoey was concerned. Oh, and his wrinkles—new ones around his eyes—made him look wise and distinguished. They added character to an already handsome face, and they looked *so* good on him. Did they come from stress, though? Zoey wondered about that as she thought about all the stress that had mounted up in his life this past year.

Anyway, as it turned out, Zoey had planned for a one-time walk only, assuming that Daniel would get bored with it, or her, and not want to come back. But that was not the way it worked out. No, not at all. In fact, midway through their jaunt, he'd told her he was eager to walk with her again. Make it a regular date, perhaps.

That did catch her by surprise and, while the prospect of having Daniel with her every time she walked excited her, it also filled her with a modest amount of trepidation as he would be seeing her in her rawest of states on a regular basis. Her walks were a no-makeup, messy-haired, dress-down kind of affair, when she honestly paid no attention to how she looked. But she wanted to look good for Daniel, and that was what worried her. Walking like she did, she couldn't present herself the way she wanted, and that was something Daniel was sure to notice. But she couldn't dress up for him for those five miles, as that would be putting on airs she truly didn't own.

Well, so be it. He'd just have to see her the

way she was and she'd have to live with the consequences.

"We could do that again," Daniel commented after they made their round of the park and ended up back at Zoey's house. He glanced at his watch—a new device that tracked his exercise, steps, movements…pretty much everything he did. "We've got plenty of time."

"Sorry, but I can't. I've got time to shower and get ready for work, and that's about all," she told him, fully intending *not* to invite him inside. It was too early in the day to get *that* involved.

Daniel must have taken the hint at the door for, as she turned her back to him and went inside, he stepped aside when her screen door almost banged into him. "I think I'll shower when I get to work. It's easier than going back home."

"But home is only a mile away."

He grinned. "Home is where my bed may call me back for another ten minutes, which will turn into twenty, which will turn into thirty, making me late to work."

"You really hate mornings, don't you?"

"I don't hate them. I just try to avoid them."

"But your job requires you to be up bright and early."

"And your walking requires me to be up even earlier."

"Then sleep in. You don't have to come with me next time I go." A small part of her wanted him to take her up on that un-invite, but a larger part of her wanted him to greet her, pulled weeds in hand, ready to walk again. Wanting and not wanting…this was beginning to be such a battle in her; she didn't know how she could keep up with it.

Zoey turned around to face Daniel, realizing that she wanted him more than she didn't want him. "This morning was…pleasant," she said, hesitantly.

"You sure won't commit to anything solid, will you?"

"Pleasant is solid enough."

"Pleasant is noncommittal. You could have told me you enjoyed spending the last thirty minutes with me, or that you look forward to walking with me again. That would have been committal."

"Committal?"

"You know…committing or entrusting."

"Well, I'm entrusting to you the task of coming back next time I walk. Are you committed to that?"

Daniel raised amused eyebrows. "Fancy words, lady."

"Your words, not mine."

"Actually, my only word is *yes*."

"Yes, as in, you'll be back?"

"Yes, as in, I'm looking forward to seeing you again."

He was lingering, on purpose, and attempting a conversation that would allow them a little more time together. It was a deliberate ploy, one she could see right through, and one she didn't mind in the least as she didn't want him to leave her quite yet. More and more, she was enjoying her time with Daniel, always mindful that it could turn into nothing. Or everything, if they could both get past their self-made obstacles. "That would be…"

"Pleasant?" he interrupted.

A smile crept to Zoey's face. "I was going to say *nice*."

"Well, that's better than pleasant."

"Look, Daniel, I don't know what you want from me. I mean, I thought we were going to be friends, but this is turning into something that goes beyond friendship. At least, you're dropping all kinds of hints that it could."

"And you're opposed to that?" he asked.

"I don't know what I am." That much was true. The further she got into this relationship with Daniel, the more confused she was getting. Was he truly ready to move on now?

Did she want to be his *first* since Elizabeth? Of course, there was still that big question that had plagued her since they'd met that day in the coffee shop: could she measure up? That, if nothing else, put a damper on any forward progress she might want to make with him. That obstacle she alone had to get past.

"How about I go away and let you figure that out? Then maybe we could have dinner sometime, once you know."

"Are we dating, Daniel?" Blunt question, but she had to ask it.

"More like skirting around dating, since I've never asked you out on a proper date. Which I would, if I thought you'd accept."

So maybe there had been no formal attempt at dating, but lately she'd spent an awful lot of time with Daniel and, to her, that was almost the same as dating. "Skirting is good," she said.

"But what if I asked you out the way most men ask women to go out? None of this chance meeting or planned activity rubbish we've been doing. Would you accept?"

"Probably," she conceded.

Daniel couldn't hide the look of surprise overtaking his face. "Is that closer to a yes or no?"

"Closer to a yes." This was so bold of her,

and so unlike her. But she liked the change happening within her. Liked it a lot.

"Then will you go out with me? Just me… no Maddie. No power walking. No hospital or patient business."

She didn't even hesitate before she answered. "Yes. I'd like that." Said with no momentary qualms, even though she knew those might set in after she'd had time to think about this.

"Friday night? Maybe we can go down to the pier and have a nice dinner, then take in the sights. You know—keep it simple."

"Simple's good," she said, preparing to shut the door. It was time to get ready for work. No more putting it off even if she would have liked to linger at the door like she was, talking awhile longer to Daniel.

He smiled and started to back away. "Well, then… Friday."

"Friday," she repeated, then closed the door. Zoey's first inclination was to hurry to the window to watch him walk down her steps, but she didn't do that, as her knees were too wobbly to carry her even that short distance. So instead, she simply leaned against the door for a minute, willing her nerves to settle down. But they didn't as, the more she thought about what she'd just now accepted, the more her nerves ran uncontrolled through her entire body. "OK, calm down, Zoey. It'll be fine."

Fine? How was this going to be fine, when her stomach was already in a knot over it? For that matter, how was this going to be fine when she knew that Elizabeth still stood as an obstacle between them?

Yeah, right. Fine! Nothing about it was fine, yet she wasn't going to do anything to stop it.

Two days to figure it out. Two days to convince himself he wasn't doing a bad thing.

Daniel sighed impatiently as he perused one of his patient's charts. He needed to change the antibiotic order as Mrs. Jenkins in Room Seven-Ten seemed to be having an allergic reaction to the one he'd prescribed earlier. She hadn't told him about her allergy until after the rash had popped up, and only then did she admit that erythromycin had caused this in her before.

"You should have told me," he mumbled as he scribbled the new order.

"Doctor?" the nurse seated next to him at the nurses' station asked.

"Sorry…talking to myself."

"Whatever keeps you sane," she told him, then turned her attention back to the notes she was charting.

Sanity…such a sketchy concept some-times. What was sanity, anyway? Sometimes he wasn't sure he knew. So had he been lack-ing in sanity when he'd asked Zoey out on a proper date? He might have been. Certainly, he'd never intended to date *anyone* so soon. In fact, his general life plan had been to wait until Maddie was older before he pursued anything. Yet his plans had been flying out the window since the first moment he'd spotted Zoey in that coffee shop.

Slowly, Daniel trudged his way back down to Mrs. Jenkins to inform her that he was changing her medication. "Any other aller-gies I should know about?" he asked.

"Peanuts," she said. "Oh, and pollen. I get bad hay fever in the spring and autumn."

She pulled her blanket up to her chin and wiggled down into the bed. "When will I get out of here, Doctor?" she asked.

Patients always wanted to go home, even be-fore they were cured. He couldn't blame them as home was where he wanted to be right now. Home playing with Maddie. Fixing her spa-ghetti. Brushing her long hair. Doing all the things Elizabeth used to do. "Day after tomor-row, if I get your rash under control."

"Could I go home and get it under control there?" she asked him.

"I want to keep an eye on you another day or so, in case the rash gets worse." His mind was totally not on Mrs. Jenkins' rash. Not on anything hospital-related.

"I really need a day off," he told Abby later that day when he went to get Maddie.

"You look tired," she replied.

"Tired of the routine."

"Daddy!" Maddie squealed, jumping into his arms as he bent down to catch her. "Can we go for pizza?"

"You're going to turn into a pizza if we're not careful," he teased.

"She needs a proper meal," Abby interjected. "Not pizza every night. Maybe I should do more cooking for her—send it with you when you come to get her."

"She gets a proper meal almost every night," Daniel said, trying to stay calm. He simply wasn't in the mood to have Abby come at him right now. Wasn't in the mood to fight back, either. It was too difficult, too painful. And Elizabeth would have hated this little back and forth he and Abby always seemed to get into. But Abby was suffering in ways he couldn't even understand. To lose her only child... His heart did break for Abby as much as his heart broke for himself. Which was why he never walked away from her. She needed her family, and he and Maddie *were* her family. "Speaking of which, could you watch her Friday night?"

"Do you have to work late?" Abby asked him.

There was no easy way to do this. No easy way to tell her that he was beginning to move forward. He didn't want to hurt her, but any way he put this he was afraid he would. "I… um… I have a date."

"A date?" Abby's face drained of all color. "I… I didn't expect that so soon, Daniel."

"Neither did I. But it just sort of happened." He sighed. "It's time, Abby. What can I say? I loved Elizabeth dearly, still do, but I need to move on with things now."

"I know you do. It's just that…things are changing so quickly. I don't have Elizabeth anymore. Maddie's growing up. And now you…" She brushed back a tear that was sliding from her eye. "Is she a nice woman, Daniel?"

"She is. In fact, you know her."

"One of Elizabeth's friends?"

"No, not one of her friends, exactly. It's her nurse, Zoey Evans."

"Zoey? I don't understand. Have you been keeping up with her all along?"

"No. I haven't seen her since Elizabeth died.

But, recently I bumped into Zoey at a coffee shop and we seemed to hit it off."

"I knew you'd move on. Elizabeth wanted you to. She told me to help you through it if I could. But, Daniel, this scares me. I've already lost Elizabeth, and the next thing you know, I'll be losing you and Maddie, too. And now that you're dating again, it seems so…close."

"You're not going to lose either one of us, Abby. We're family, and that's not going to change."

"But if you remarry…where does that leave me?"

"The same place you've always been—important to us. Nothing I will do in the future is going to change that. Maddie needs you because you're her grandmother, and I need you because we're both so connected to Elizabeth, and that's something only the two of us can share."

"Then you won't take Maddie away from me? Because I love having her with me every day. Love that more than anything else in my life."

"No, I'm not taking Maddie away from you."

"Even if you marry a woman who doesn't want me around because I'm your first wife's mother?"

"First off, I'm not getting married right now.

Not even thinking about it, as I haven't even dated. But in the future, if I do marry again, it will be to someone who accepts you as part of my family. Because you are." Daniel leaned over and pulled Abby into his arms. "But you are going to have to quit spoiling Maddie the way you do."

"I spoil her?"

He chuckled. "Quite a lot. And, while I know grandmothers have the right to spoil a grandchild a little bit, you're way out there with Maddie. Once in a while, tell her no. Don't always give in to what she wants. Don't think that you have to earn her love with the things you give her, because she's going to love you just because you're her grandmother."

"But I want her to have everything."

"So did Elizabeth and I, but we also wanted Maddie to be strong and independent, and it's hard for that to happen when she's got you to fall back on. You taught Elizabeth how to be strong and independent and, whatever you did for her, that's what I want you to do for Maddie. She needs that from you, Abby. Because, apart from me, you're the only other connection to her mother she'll ever have, and I want her to get to know Elizabeth through you." This was the talk that Zoey had suggested he have, and he felt good about it. It *was* time for him to move forward with Abby, without resentment. "Anyway, can you watch Maddie for me Friday night, or do I have to find another babysitter?"

"Of course I can watch Maddie. And I hope you and Zoey have a nice time. She was so good to my Elizabeth…"

Restless. That was what she was feeling tonight. Restless and apprehensive. And excited, as well. Daniel certainly caused a mix of emotions in her, and she wondered how someone could both dread and look forward to a simple date.

It wasn't like she'd never dated before, even though that was what this felt like—a total first date scenario. Honestly, she'd never felt this way with her husband. No breathless anticipation. No real excitement. "So what was I thinking when I married him?" she asked her mother in an uncharacteristic midweek phone call.

"You were probably thinking with your hormones," her mother said. "The way all young people do nowadays."

Zoey thought back to the weeks leading up to her wedding, and she couldn't remember an abundance of hormones in action. Or maybe she didn't want to remember them. Either way, she'd been attracted to Brad. He was a handsome man. Smooth-talking. Sophisticated. But her desires hadn't overwhelmed her the way her desires toward Daniel had. "That was a long time ago. I don't exactly remember."

"Are they kicking up again?" her mother went on. "Is that why you're so nervous about dating this young man?"

She wasn't sure she could sum up her nervousness in a simple explanation, as she didn't really understand it herself. "No. His wife was one of my patients and, even though I didn't notice him so much then, it all changed when I met up with him recently."

"Changed as in…?"

"I really like the guy, Mom. He's nice to me. Attentive. Fun to talk to. Nothing at all like Brad."

"They don't all turn out to be Brad, dear. Let's hope this man you're about to start dating is one of the good ones."

"His name is Daniel. And, yes, I think he *is* one of the good ones," Zoey admitted.

"Don't get my hopes up," her mother warned. "You're not getting any younger, you know. And neither am I. So I'm keeping my fingers crossed that you'll find yourself in a happy relationship that gets you married and pregnant."

"You're being premature, since this is our first real date, and I have no idea how it's going to turn out."

"But one date leads to another."

"Maybe." She wasn't quite ready to see herself in a second date picture. Even though she and Daniel had been together a lot these past weeks, she'd never considered what they'd been doing together as dating. So, in Zoey's mind, a dinner at the pier on Friday night was indeed a first date. That was as far as she allowed herself to think ahead. "But we'll have to wait and see how the first one turns out."

"Since you nursed his wife, I assume he's a widower. So, does he have children?"

"A three-year-old daughter."

"Then I could be a grandmother sooner than I thought!"

"Hold on. You're jumping way ahead."

"Just planning my future," her mother said cheerfully.

"Well, don't plan too hard. I haven't even been on a first date yet."

"Do you like this Daniel enough to think about having a future with him? Maybe not married for now, but something serious?"

"I do like him. Very much. The thing that worries me, though, is that he's still quite connected to his wife, so I don't know how that could turn into anything for me." Zoey settled back into her sofa and kicked up her feet. Even though they had their moments of disagreement, it was nice talking to her mother about this. Nice having a real mother-to-daughter chat. "But like I said, I like him more than I probably should, considering the circumstances."

"Tell me about those circumstances, dear," her mother said. "Anything you're comfortable with."

Sighing, Zoey dropped her head back onto the sofa cushions. "Well, it all started a year ago when I was assigned to take care of…" Shutting her eyes, she continued the story, starting with the first time she'd met Daniel and ending with today. When she finally hung up the phone, she was exhausted emotionally. But satisfied. And for the first time, hopeful, because the story she'd just told her mother seemed like it should have a happy ending. Whether or not it would was yet to be determined, but for now she was content to let her new-found hopefulness embrace her.

He didn't normally pay much attention to his appearance anymore. At work he wore scrubs. Any place else, he wore jeans and whatever shirt or sweater he pulled out of his closet.

Today was different, though. He wanted to look good for Zoey.

Daniel found a pair of nice khaki trousers in the back of the closet and wondered if they still fit him. He'd been all over the place with his weight this past year—down, then back up. Honestly, he didn't know where these trousers belonged in his transition, so he tried them on and decided they looked decent enough. The long-sleeved, blue-striped dress shirt looked pretty good on him, too. So he was set. Casual and stylish. At least he hoped he was, as the last time he'd cared about his appearance he'd had someone to critique him on it.

This wasn't easy, moving on the way he was doing. Seeing Zoey on a non-date was one thing, but an honest-to-goodness date with her? One he'd actually declared a date? No, it wasn't easy at all, because it was the first step in letting go, which seemed to be a big problem for him.

*"Go on without me, Daniel..."*

Of course he'd told Abby it was time, and maybe he was right to heed his own words. And Elizabeth's words. Maybe it *was* time. After all, who drew the line in the sand that marked the moment when someone was supposed to step over it and forge ahead?

*Put away the guilt*, Daniel warned himself

as he checked out his appearance in the bathroom mirror. *It's going to ruin your evening. It's going to ruin Zoey's evening.*

Damn, he wished he had Elizabeth here to talk to. She'd have known how he was supposed to progress. But she wasn't here, and her voice was beginning to fade away.

"Our reservation is for seven thirty," Daniel told Zoey. "So we've got some time to kill before we need to leave."

"Care for some wine? Or a soft drink?" Daniel looked nervous. Almost as nervous as she was feeling.

"Wine would be good," he said. "In the kitchen, or in here?"

What was she thinking? She hadn't offered him a seat. "Please, sit on the couch. It's more comfortable than my kitchen chairs."

"Well, you saw my couch the other night, all stained with grape juice and spaghetti sauce," he said. "Which is why I normally take people straight out to the kitchen."

"The perils of having a three-year-old…" She stopped talking, blinked, then sighed. "Why are we both so nervous?" she finally asked him. "I mean, it's not like we haven't been seeing each other for a while, because we've been seeing each other everywhere."

"I guess attaching the tag 'official date' to what we're doing is the reason."

"Are you ready to date again, Daniel?" she asked bluntly.

"I think I am."

"But you're not sure."

"Does that offend you? Because I didn't mean for it to."

"No, I'm not offended. And I'm glad you can be honest about your feelings, because I know this can't be easy for you."

"I didn't used to be so damned tentative. Back when I met Elizabeth, I was pretty bold. Asked her out the same day I met her. None of this hesitating, like we're doing."

And so Elizabeth was creeping back in. "I don't see you as tentative so much as I see you being cautious."

"'Cautious' is a polite way to put it."

"Then why did you ask me out? Why move past what we've already established between us and risk it not working?"

"Are you satisfied where we are?"

The directness of Daniel's question caught Zoey off-guard as she'd never thought about the two of them in terms of being satisfied. "Maybe not satisfied so much as accepting." Before he could probe any deeper, she hurried off to the kitchen to fetch the wine, and returned a few minutes later holding two goblets half-full of a white Zinfandel. "I hope this is OK. I should have asked you, since I do have a nice Burgundy open, as well."

"It's fine," he said, taking his glass. "So, why don't you sit down and try to relax for a little while, instead of running around, trying to stay away from me?"

"I'm not trying to stay away from you," she defended, even though she wondered if that was exactly what she was doing.

"But you're not trying to stay close, either."

"Daniel, you know I have qualms about the two of us. I mean, I don't want to, but I can't help that it's happening."

"Yet we keep coming back together, and you do nothing to stop that."

So true. She wasn't trying to put an end to them. "Do you want to stop it?" she asked him.

"No."

"Neither do I."

"Then we keep going on the way we are, nervous and tentative? Me afraid to move ahead, you afraid of me?"

"That's not how I want it, Daniel. But it's the way it seems to work out." Zoey sat down, but not too close to him. "It's like we're the right people but we're one step out of time."

She took a sip of her wine, taking care not

to spill any, as her hands were shaking slightly when she raised the glass to her lips. "And I don't know how to take the step that will put us back in time together."

"It's funny how we can see the problem but can't find a way to fix it."

"Maybe that's because neither one of us is sure we want it fixed."

And again, it was back to Elizabeth. She should have been angry, but she wasn't. More like she was just sad. Sad for her. Sad for Daniel. Sad for what they might want yet couldn't reach out and grab on to.

# CHAPTER TEN

SOMEWHERE BETWEEN THE house salad and the seafood Newburg, Zoey mentioned wall climbing and how she looked forward to doing it on Saturday mornings a couple of times a month. Her description of how she scaled the wall caught Daniel's attention because he didn't take his eyes off her for even a moment of it. Then, somewhere between the seafood Newburg and the cheesecake, she'd asked him if he'd like to go with her. Tomorrow morning. Bright and early to beat the crowds. Bring Maddie, she'd said. They'd have a nice brunch somewhere afterward.

Daniel had agreed, quite eagerly. So now here he was, on their first real date, sitting on a public bench with Zoey at the dock, at night, both of them watching a tug boat make its way slowly to the harbor, while he was wondering how much of a fool he was going to make of himself the next morning. It wasn't inevitable that he was going to come off as clumsy to Zoey, since he did have a fair amount of athletic skill in his background. But all that was a long time ago, and he was so out of practice at almost everything now, he was worried that what should probably come easily would not. Quite honestly, he didn't want to make a fool of himself in front of her.

Out of practice but not out of shape, he reminded himself, thinking of all the grueling physical hours he put in at the hospital. Those were a workout in themselves, which was good, considering he didn't have much time to get to the gym.

Still, spending a Saturday morning with Zoey... He was excited by the prospect no matter what form it took. "Are you sure you want me along?" he asked, keeping his fingers crossed she wouldn't have seconds thoughts. "Because I might embarrass you."

"I really want you to come. I mean, you don't have to, if you don't want to. But I thought you might enjoy it since it'll be something new for you. You don't have other plans, do you?"

"Not in the morning. Maddie wants to come down to the pier in the afternoon and throw bread to the seagulls, though. But that's all I have on the schedule, so I'm...*we're*...free in the morning."

"Well, I don't climb all day. Usually an hour or so does it for me. And, like I said, if we have time we can catch a brunch somewhere afterward."

"Brunch sounds good."

"Well, the restaurant I have in mind sets up a nice little buffet table for children, so I'll bet we'll be able to convince her to eat something."

"You thought of Maddie when you were planning this?" He was genuinely touched that she was considerate enough to include his child in the plans.

"She counts, too, you know. I think a lot of people overlook kids, sort of lump them into the group with everybody else, or forget that they have their own preferences. But they do, so I figured she'd like a buffet that serves spaghetti, pizza and chicken nuggets. All kids' favorites."

Daniel leaned over and kissed Zoey on the cheek, then wrapped his arm around her shoulders. "Thank you," he whispered. "One of the toughest aspects of getting back into the swing of a social life is finding a place for Maddie there. We come as a package deal and I have a really big fear that some people—a woman I might date, for instance—would be put off by that."

"Those are the people who don't deserve to be your friend. Anyone who would be *put off* by a child... I guess I don't understand that. To know you is to know that Maddie is a huge part of who you are. If they don't accept her, they don't accept you."

"But it's a very real fear for a lot of single parents. I have a friend at the hospital, another doctor, who was dating someone he believed could be his next wife. That is, until she asked him if he would send his son off to a boarding school so they could have more time alone together."

"It ruined the relationship, didn't it?"

"As well as his desire to date again. That was three years ago, and he's turned into a social hermit, kind of like me."

"You're not a social hermit, Daniel. Not totally."

He chuckled. "But I'm damned close to it, and even you'll have to admit that."

Sighing, Zoey leaned her head against him. "What I'll admit is that you're a little bumpy at the starting gate. But I don't think that, when the gate's fully open to you, Maddie will hold you back. You're too good of a parent to get involved with someone who doesn't want her around."

"Maddie coming first in my life doesn't bother you, does it?"

"What would bother me is if she *didn't* come first. Look, where I go climbing they have a small wall, just a few feet off the ground, for children. It's only a few hand-holds high, but it does give the children a feel for a real wall. I thought Maddie might enjoy trying that once she sees us climbing."

"You've thought of everything to take care of my daughter, haven't you?"

"I want Maddie to have as much fun as you'll have climbing."

"I appreciate that." Dinner had been lovely and right now he felt as contented as he'd felt in a long time. They'd successfully avoided talking about their relationship and instead listened to each other's stories of home and family and things that had taken place in their lives, all of it very nice. "Even if we put Maddie on the wall, don't you think an hour of climbing sounds like a long time to be suspending yourself from ropes?"

"It'll go by faster than you think. And I promise you'll love it!" Zoey said enthusiastically. "One of these days I hope to scale a real rock outside somewhere, and not one set up in a warehouse."

"As in mountain climbing?"

"In my future, maybe."

"By any chance, do you ski? Because I love to ski, and maybe we can do it together sometime." Here he was now, making plans into their future. And, surprisingly, not overcome with enormous guilt. More than that, the fact that he didn't feel guilty didn't *make him* feel guilty. Times were changing.

"Ah, a part of your world."

"A nice part. I used to try to go out several times during the winter. Go up to Canada, actually, where they have some amazing ski runs."

"You and Elizabeth?"

He shook his head no. "She hated the slopes. But I tried to change her mind. Got her out with me one day, but she refused to leave the ski lodge." He chuckled, remembering Elizabeth's stubbornness. Once she'd put her foot down, there'd been no changing her mind. Like mother like daughter, as Maddie had the same trait. "Instead, she stayed back and sipped hot cocoa."

"Not me! I'd be out there, making a fool of myself, since I've never skied. So now do you take Maddie when you go?"

"I haven't. Last time I skied was before Elizabeth got sick, and Maddie was only a baby then. But I'm hoping to get her out there this year and introduce her to one of the beginner runs."

"Would Elizabeth have allowed that?"

"As much as she refused for herself, I don't think she would have held Maddie back. At least, until Maddie herself expressed her like or dislike of an activity. She was very openminded about those types of things as far as Maddie was concerned."

"Maddie's like her, isn't she?"

"Very much. She looks like her, acts like her, but the hell of it is I'm not even sure she has that much memory of her."

"By the time I knew Elizabeth she was too sick to take part in much parenting. I wish that I could have seen more of her being Maddie's mother."

"She was born for it," Daniel said as a sadness settled into his eyes. But, he shook it off immediately with an actual physical shake of his body. "Anyway, about skiing... Do you want to come with us sometime this winter?"

"Winter's a long ways off."

"I like to plan ahead." And planning ahead with Zoey was taking a big leap of faith that they'd have more than tonight and tomorrow together. Daniel pulled her tighter into him and bent to whisper in her ear, "And, since you've never skied, I'm going to love teaching you."

"After I teach *you* how to climb a rock."

Nuzzling into her hair, he noted the faint trace of strawberry shampoo. It was a nice, sensual smell. "Give me a few minutes on the wall, and I'll bet I'll beat you up the next time."

Zoey laughed. "That competitive, are you?"

"Either competitive or foolish."

"So, do you want to make an actual wager on that?"

"Sure. One more date. If I win, you have to go. If you win, the decision to go or not is up to you."

"If I go, I get to choose the place."

"Agreed. And if I lose, I get to challenge you one more time to try and win that date."

"But if you lose, my choice might be to have that date anyway."

"Then it's a win-win for me. I get one, maybe even two dates with you, no matter how it turns out." That was the kind of wager he liked.

"But, if you win the second time, can I re-challenge you?"

"That could mean a third date, you know."

"I think I can live with that."

Sighing, Daniel tilted his head back on the park bench and looked up at the dark sky above, feeling so mellow he wanted to melt into the night. This was turning into such a lovely evening that he didn't want it to be over with. "For a first *real* date, this was...nice," he said. "I'm glad that we both fought our demons to get us here."

"Big demons," she said.

"But I think they're shrinking."

"I hope so, Daniel. I really hope so."

"Are you up for a walk down to the docks? I like to watch the late-night fishermen go out." Dreading that he would lose the sensual feel of her pressed to his body, yet wanting so badly to walk with her hand in hand along the pier—a romantic image he couldn't get out of his head—he shifted slightly more in to Zoey. "They bring their haul in early in the morning and turn it over to the mongers to sell. I've been tempted to come down here some morning and buy something, but Maddie hates fish, so it would be a waste of time and money."

"I love fresh fish," Zoey said, leaning her head against his shoulder. "And I love late-night walks along the pier. Not that I've ever done that before, because I haven't. But I'm sure..."

He silenced her with his finger to her lips. And smiled. "I'm sure, too," he whispered, bending forward to kiss her.

Daniel's touch was light at first. No probing, no pressing, no urgency. Just simply his lips to hers, heads tilted, mouths open. Blending to each other perfectly as he pulled her even closer.

Zoey yielded her mouth to his kiss, loving the way his tongue lightly tickled her lower lip. The feel of him was almost decadent, and in that sensation lay buried a world of deepness, of sensuality, she'd never before imagined. As she tickled his lip with her tongue, it was all she could do to keep herself reined in. But they stayed light for a time, existing in a place where exploration was so near, yet so far away.

"We're pretty good at this," she whispered, pulling slightly back from him. Wondering, for an instant, if he was conflicted at all by what he was doing.

His eyes sought hers in a deep, abiding gaze. Then he smiled. "*Very* good."

Those were the only words she needed to hear as she pushed herself back into him and pressed her mouth hard to his.

Daniel parted her willing lips with his tongue and delved inside, meeting her probing tongue on its journey to him. Moaning, he pressed even harder until there was no separation between them. They were breathing the same breath, their hearts beating in perfect synchronization.

For Zoey, every kiss that had come before Daniel was now gone. Vanished. Forgotten.

Their moment ended when a foghorn from a distant lighthouse sounded its warning. Daniel was the first to pull away from it, regretting that they had to be separated. But they did. At least, *he* did, as his feelings were about to explode. He was falling in love with her, pure and simple. It wasn't something he'd expected would happen so soon. Wasn't something he'd necessarily wanted to happen. But there he was, sitting on the pier, holding the most glorious woman in his arms and not sure what to do about it other than defer the moment. Defer the emotions until he could figure out what to do with them. Defer his happiness. "Maybe some morning, instead of a walk, we could come down here and do a little shopping for something to cook after work."

Zoey snapped her eyes wide open and looked puzzled over this sudden change in direction. But she regained herself quickly. "Right. Our morning walk. Um…do the mongers here sell to the individual public, or do the fish go mostly to restaurants and markets?" She reached up and brushed her finger to her lips.

Even her slightest gesture was sensual. Everything about Zoey Evans was sensual which made him suddenly feel out of step again. Damn it, he wanted that to go away. Didn't want it always coming back to plague him. Not now. Not ever again. "The restaurants and markets get their pick, but there are a few stalls that open up to the public."

Zoey cleared her throat and sat up straight, her body language a clear indication that their intimacy had ended. "You know, I think I'll take a rain check on that walk. It's late, and I have some reading to do before I go to bed. So I'd better be getting home to get things sorted so I'll be up to beating you on the wall in the morning."

Well, he'd gone and blown that one, hadn't he? What the hell was wrong with him, anyway?

Zoey scooted away from him and broke their embrace, but she did reach back over and took hold of his hand. "Dinner was lovely. The whole evening was lovely."

There it was. The official *you turned me off* verbiage. Zoey was clearly done with their evening, and there was nothing he could do to change that except kick himself.

"I really messed it up, didn't I?" Of course, she wouldn't tell him that he had. She was too kind to do that.

"Let's just say that the evening went as far as it could go, and leave it at that, OK?" She stood up and waited for him to do the same. "And don't blame yourself for anything because, for your first time really getting out there, I think you did quite well."

"You don't have to soft-pedal me, Zoey. I know exactly how *well* I did." He knew exactly how he'd turned a pleasant evening into a disaster, and this time there were no doubts about anything. What he wanted and what he could have weren't necessarily the same thing. Damn it, anyway!

"Wow," Maddie said, looking up at her daddy. She took a step backward and reached for Zoey's hand. "What's he doing up there?"

"Trying to get to the top."

"Why?" Maddie asked.

"To see what's up there."

"Why?" the child asked again.

"Because he doesn't know and he wants to find out."

"Why?" she asked for a third time.

"Because he's never been all the way to the top before." Maddie had been a little chatterbox ever since Daniel had strapped on the ropes, and Zoey was surprised by how un-shy she was. The Maddie she'd known a year ago, while she hadn't had a mastery of much language yet, had always clung to her mother's bedside, hiding her face. And the Maddie she'd encountered recently with Daniel had been very stubborn. But this child... she was totally outgoing. Happy. Inquisitive. A real delight. "He's waving to you, Maddie. So wave back."

Maddie hoisted her little arm above her head and gave her daddy a hearty wave. "What can Daddy see?" she asked Zoey.

"Right now he can see you." Zoey wanted to be enthused, but it was difficult, considering the way their night out had ended. She'd paced the floor an hour after Daniel had dropped her off, then tossed and turned in her bed for another hour before she'd finally dropped off into a fitful sleep. Things had been going so nicely, then all of a sudden he'd pulled back. She had to wonder if it was his guilt doing that, or if he was deciding it was easier to not get involved. Either way, it had her worried. "And he's still waving. See?"

"He has to come down now," Maddie said in all seriousness. "Because I want to climb."

Zoey had shown Maddie the child's climbing wall when Daniel was gearing up, and Maddie had wanted to climb it then and there. She was a lot like Daniel, in that respect. Adventurous. Outgoing. He was doing a good job with her, and it showed. "He'll be down in a minute."

"Then I'm going to climb!" the child said emphatically.

Zoey had her phone camera ready to take pictures, the way she'd taken pictures of Daniel getting ready to climb, then climbing, and now was snapping picture of his descent. He'd surprised her with his ability. For someone who'd never scaled a wall before, he'd done a good job of it. Much better than she'd expected. And, yes, on their second attempt, he'd beat her to the top, which meant he had a date coming. If he wanted another date. After last night, she wasn't sure.

"That was fun," he said, not in the least winded as he unfastened his helmet strap once he was back on the ground. "Looks like I get another date!" Before Zoey could respond to that, he tousled his daughter's hair and asked, "You ready to climb, Maddie?"

"Not that one, Daddy." She pointed at the child's wall. "That one."

"I told her it was just her size."

Daniel handed his helmet and harnesses back to the attendant then took hold of Maddie's other hand—the one Zoey wasn't still holding on to. It was an intimate little snapshot—one, Zoey believed, that would make them look like the perfect family to anyone who was looking on. Stupid snapshot, she thought. Especially since two of the people in it didn't know what they wanted.

"Can I climb it, too?" he asked Maddie.

"No, silly! You're too big." She giggled as she pulled away from Daniel and Zoey and ran toward the wall.

"I think she likes this," Daniel said, looking over the tops of other children's heads to keep an eye on his daughter.

"Will you do this again with her?"

"With you, too, I hope."

"Are you sure, Daniel? Because after last night…"

"Remember when you said we were fighting some big demons, and I said they were shrinking?"

Zoey nodded.

"Well, it seems like mine aren't shrinking as much as I thought they were. I'm sorry about last night, Zoey. Look at the bags under my eyes and that will tell you how much I didn't sleep, because I was so upset."

"I lost some sleep, too," she admitted.

"Can you be patient with me? I know where I'm wrong, and I'm trying to fix it, but it's not happening as easily as I thought it would."

"You mean getting over Elizabeth?"

"Not getting over her. But getting on without her. Moving in a new direction, taking on a new life."

"Keep in mind that I'm taking on a new life here, too, Daniel. And sure, it's more difficult for you than it is for me, but that doesn't diminish the fact that I'm struggling along with you."

Daniel reached over and took her hand. "I know," he said. "I really do know."

She knew, too. But what she didn't know was if they'd make it through. Daniel had already had his perfectly suited wife, and Maddie was a testament to their happiness. It was beautiful to watch, though, and beautiful to dream that she could find her place there. But could she really? Or would Daniel, at some point, draw his line and keep her on the other side of it?

"Are you going all the way to the top?" she asked Maddie, trying to take her mind off the hopelessness overtaking her.

Daniel turned and winked at Zoey. "Not only is she going all the way to the top, she's going to do it faster than Daddy did."

Maddie tugged Daniel toward the wall whilst Zoey stood back and aimed her camera, ready to shoot multiple pictures of them.

"Look at me and smile," she called out when Maddie was finally standing face-first to the gray, rock-shaped wall, ready to start climbing.

Both father and daughter smiled for the camera, but only for a second, as Maddie had already grasped her first hand-hold. Then the second. Then her feet were off the ground. Naturally, Daniel was there to support her, keeping his hand firmly in the square of her back.

"Good job, Maddie!" Zoey called out as the child reached the halfway point. Of course, she clicked off a picture of that milestone. Then another when Maddie reached the top and threw her hands into the air in celebration.

As her hands went up, Maddie started to lurch backward, but Daniel had a firm hold on her and kept her upright and in place. So after Maddie waved to Zoey, then had a good look down at the ground, she started her descent. A little too quickly, probably, as Daniel had to take over guiding her to the floor. None of that mattered to Maddie, though. She'd made her conquest and her victory was written all over her face.

"That was amazing!" Zoey said when Maddie ran over to her once Daniel had removed her climbing gear.

"I was faster than Daddy!" the child exclaimed, taking hold of Zoey's hand. "Can I do it again?"

"Next time, sweetheart," Daniel said.

"When?"

"Next Saturday, if I'm not called into work."

"Can Zoey come, too?"

Daniel raised amused eyebrows at Zoey. "Can you come, too?" he asked, smiling. "And before you answer, let me just state that my daughter doesn't make these kinds of requests lightly. She likes to keep me to herself when she has the chance."

"Then maybe I shouldn't interfere." Even though the prospect of another climb with Daniel felt promising.

"Actually, I kind of liked showing off for the fair lady."

"You mean showing *up* the fair lady?"

"Did I hurt your feelings?" Daniel asked. His dimples accentuated his bright eyes when he smiled.

"Just my pride."

"Well, your pride can have another crack at me next week."

"Somehow, I don't think my pride stands a chance with you." *Nothing* about her stood a chance where Daniel was concerned. And, yes, she would be patient for Daniel, because that was the only promise she had to hold on to.

# CHAPTER ELEVEN

ZOEY GLANCED AT the caller ID on her phone and her heart automatically skipped a beat. Daniel. "Didn't I just leave you a couple of hours ago?" she asked, rather than answering with a cheery hello. They'd walked together earlier. They hadn't said much. Mostly just walked. And she'd wondered why Daniel had seemed so preoccupied.

"So, sue me. I wanted to hear your voice."

Her heart skipped yet another beat. "It hasn't changed since this morning. And I'm reasonably sure this morning's voice will be the same as tomorrow morning's voice. So, what's your real reason for calling?"

"I thought we might have dinner together tonight. Maddie's going to spend the night with her grandmother, which means it will be only the two of us."

"Then I'm your back-up plan when Maddie's not there to keep you entertained?" They hadn't been out, with or without Maddie, since that day on the rock-climbing wall a week ago, and she'd been beginning to wonder if he was ever going to ask her out again.

"Are you going to make this difficult on me?"

Zoey arched amused eyebrows, even though Daniel wasn't there to gauge her expression. "I'm not going to make it any more difficult on you than you do on me."

"How do I make it difficult on you?"

Something about the lack of intimacy on a phone put her off, so she didn't tell him that the way they'd established their relationship was frazzling her nerves. And she didn't tell him that she needed a clearer idea of where they were going, or where he wanted to take this thing between them. No, she didn't tell him any of that, even though he needed to know. "You interrupt me at work," she said, rather than blurting out all her concerns.

"Everybody needs a distraction now and then."

"What I *need* is to re-start an IV and get some new medicines hung."

"So how about I pick you up around seven, and we can decide where we want to go then?"

"How about you come over around seven and we stay in tonight?" She had to have a serious talk with him before she got in any deeper, and it certainly would never happen in a public restaurant.

"Sounds good. Want me to bring something?"

"No, I'll cook…well…I'll try to cook." Maybe she'd make a salad or some grilled cheese sandwiches. Certainly, he'd had better with Elizabeth, but she wasn't Elizabeth, and she didn't have any particular prowess in the kitchen. But Zoey wasn't going to let that bother her. Wasn't going to let anything about Elizabeth bother her tonight.

Daniel chuckled. "I guess I should say I'm looking forward to it."

"You may change your mind when you eat my food," she cautioned, already skipping ahead in her mind to tonight. Would they finally make a firm commitment to being together as a real couple, or would they leave it as it was, hopping and skipping over everything between them that could have real substance?

"I'll bring wine," he stated.

"Better make that two bottles. I may need to drink a lot."

Daniel stuffed his cell phone back into his pocket and headed up to the fifth floor to check on a patient who'd been admitted to the hospital the day prior with non-specific abdominal pains. He'd already ruled out appendicitis and viral gastroenteritis, and now he was considering some kind of intestinal infection such as giardia, since the man had recently traveled to a remote jungle village in South America where the water probably wasn't clean. So, stopping by the nurses' station before he went to his patient's room, he typed some test orders in his patient's chart then looked up, effectively staring blankly at the wall for the next minute. Trying to think, unable to focus.

"Doctor?"

Daniel blinked hard, shaking himself out of his near-trance-like state. "Excuse me?" he said to the nurse.

"I said, your patient's still down in X-ray. They have a shortage of transportation attendants right now and they don't anticipate bringing him back up to his room for at least another twenty minutes."

"Thank you," Daniel said absently, then headed back to the elevators and on down to his office.

Once inside, he locked the door. Something he never did when he was in there. But he'd been thinking about this moment for a few days now, and he needed to be alone. No one to disturb him, no thoughts to distract him.

"I've got to do it," he said to Elizabeth's photo as he sat down in the chair behind his desk. "This hanging in limbo with Zoey is killing both of us." He could feel it in his heart. And he could see it in Zoey's eyes every time he looked at her. So much hesitancy, so much wondering... It was taking a toll on everything in his life. Everything in Zoey's life.

Sighing, Daniel leaned back in his chair and closed his eyes. It was too early in the day for such a weariness to be setting in, but he was down-to-the-bone weary, and it had nothing at all to do with his physical condition and everything to do with his emotional shape. Bottom line: he was a mess. Conflicted. Confused. Angry at himself for everything he was putting off. For everything he was about to lose if he wasn't careful.

"I love her, Elizabeth," he confessed. "I didn't know it could happen to me again, but it did, and I want it so badly. And it didn't happen because I'm not lonely without you anymore; I have been and I still am. But this is different. It's a new beginning for me and I want to grab it and hold onto it. God help me, I *am* going on without you, Elizabeth." Just as

Elizabeth had wanted. And now, finally, just as he wanted.

Slowly, Daniel opened his eyes and looked at Elizabeth's photo again. A sad smile crept to his face as he reached out to stroke it, the way he'd stroked it so often these past months. Only this time, his stroke didn't linger. Rather, it turned into a grasp. "Damn," he whispered as he picked up the photo and held it in midair for a moment. He hadn't anticipated it being this difficult. But one simple gesture was turning into such a heartache.

As tough as this was, however, it was also the right thing to do, and the right time in which to do it. Yet, so many memories were flooding back. Memories that threatened to stop him. Memories he forced himself to blank out as he allowed himself one last look... One last touch, he thought, when he finally placed the photo into his desk drawer.

He didn't shut the drawer right away, though. No; he left it open and stared at it for an eternity, wondering if he could take the next step. This whole letting go *was* a progression of steps.

"Do it," he whispered to himself. "Do it for Zoey." Do it for any chance of a life he hoped to have with her.

But it wasn't easy. His wedding ring was

so much a part of him now that taking it off would be like cutting off his arm.

Once, his ring had been a symbol of so much hope. Now, though, it was a simply a reminder of a life that was finished. *I can do this*, he thought to himself as he twisted his ring the way he'd twisted it so many times over the past year.

One little twist...that was all he needed. Just one little twist over his knuckle and on down to the end of his finger. This had been such a long journey for him to end it this way, but this was where it had to end. So, taking in a deep breath and holding it, Daniel twisted his ring one last time then took it off and dropped it in the drawer on top of Elizabeth's photo.

He looked down at the white streak on his finger where his ring used to be, then he shut the desk drawer, laid his head down on his desk and cried.

He was standing on her front porch, illuminated by the yellow porch light, thrusting two bottles of wine at her when she opened the door. "Seriously?" she asked.

"You asked for two, I brought two." Daniel grinned. "Did you want more?"

"If I'd asked for a new sports car, would you have brought that, too?"

"I think a red one would be nice. Or would you prefer something in blue?"

Daniel looked good. Tight jeans. A nice gray T-shirt that accented his musculature. Hair a bit mussed. Dimples definitely turned on for the occasion. "I think one bottle of wine is all we'll be needing."

"Well, then, we'll put the other one away for next time." He stepped into the house and Zoey shut the door behind him. "Which I hope will be Friday night."

"Another date?" she asked him. "Before we've officially started this one?"

"Like I've told you before, I like to plan ahead."

So did she, and her mind was already racing forward. Two dates in one week…the prospect excited her and made her nervous at the same time. "Don't expect me to cook for you again. I struggled over this meal, and once in a week is enough."

He took a step closer to her, then reached out and stroked her face with the back of his hand. "What I expect is that food probably won't matter to us a whole lot by the time Friday rolls around."

Immediately, Zoey's heart started pounding hard in her chest. The implication was hers to do with as she wanted. He'd laid it out on the table for her and her choice was either to pick it up or leave it alone. "What's going on here, Daniel?" she managed to ask without sounding too breathless.

"Besides having dinner?"

"You know what I mean," she said coyly.

"I do know what you mean." He headed into the kitchen, put the bottles of wine in the fridge then turned around to Zoey, who'd followed him in. "It's all I've been thinking about for days. I mean, I've lost sleep. And it's hard to concentrate at work."

"Why?" she asked, her voice almost a whisper.

"Because it's the hardest thing I've ever had to do, yet at the same time, the easiest. I mean, I didn't expect you in my life, Zoey. I wasn't prepared for it, and I wasn't ready for it. But you happened to me and I was caught so... so unready. And I've been resisting you because of that. You know I have." He pulled out a chair at the kitchen table for Zoey then sat down across from her.

"When Elizabeth and I married, it was for ever. We had that written into our vows. And, dear God, I loved that woman so much. She came out of nowhere and changed everything in my life. Gave me a new perspective, a new outlook on life. Gave me Maddie. And, Zoey, this was a relationship I thought I didn't deserve. But I was so grateful for it because I liked the man I was with Elizabeth."

She admired his heartfelt words, but they didn't exactly instill confidence in her. In fact, they sounded to Zoey like this was the beginning and the end for them. "She loved you with that same passion, Daniel."

He smiled. "I know. In fact, we never let a day go by that we didn't acknowledge that in one way or another."

"Which is why you're having trouble moving forward in your life now. You've had perfection once, and you don't think it's out there to be found again."

"That's not true. Actually, for a while I thought it was. But these past few weeks with you… Zoey, they've been amazing. They've changed my thinking in ways you can't even begin to imagine."

This was it. This was where Daniel walked away. "But they're over now."

"No," he said quite gently, reaching across the table to take her hand. "They're not. Not if you don't want them to be."

"Then what, Daniel? I need to know what we're doing, because I can't do this anymore. I can't spend my life wondering who we are and what's going to happen with us."

"We're a couple of people stuck in a place we haven't been able to get past."

"Elizabeth…" she whispered.

"What about Elizabeth?"

"I can't compete."

"Who says you have to?"

"You do, Daniel. In the loving way you talk about her, in the way your eyes go all soft when her name is mentioned. In everything that you said just now."

"That's my transition, Zoey. You have to know where I'm coming from before we can go forward together. And I do want us to go forward together. What I'm allowing myself to discover is that you're on my mind more and more every day. And when I close my eyes, it's your image I see, not Elizabeth's. It's you I want to be with, not Elizabeth's memory, because her memories are my past and you're my future, I hope." Daniel let go of Zoey's hand, leaned back in his chair and stared across the table at her for a moment. "I took off my wedding ring today."

She glanced down at his hand and saw that his ring finger was bare. For the first time since he'd walked though her door, her hopes raised. "Are you sure you're ready for that?"

"I am. It wasn't easy, but I didn't try talking myself out of it the way I might have done a few weeks ago, because what I've finally realized is that, while Elizabeth was once my new direction and my hope for the future, that's now done. You're my new direction, my new hope, and I don't want to lose that." He leaned back across the table, took hold of her hand again and kissed her palm. "I don't want to lose you. But every time we're together you seem to pull away a little more than you did the time before."

Now her head was spinning. But she was no longer frightened. "I've been holding myself back, Daniel. At first it was because I thought I feared men, feared getting involved with someone who could hurt me again. But then we became involved, not totally immersed in it as we might have been, but involved nonetheless. Then I feared that you couldn't get over Elizabeth which, in the end, would leave me hurt."

"I can't get over Elizabeth," he admitted. "But what I can do is put my relationship with her in its proper place."

"Which is where?"

"Tucked away deep in my heart. See, my marriage wasn't like yours to Brad. You were glad to walk away from it. But I was left incomplete when my marriage was put to an end. For a while, I didn't know how to deal with that, or if I even wanted to deal with it. It's not easy being left with a big, gaping hole. It's not a good way to spend your life, and I was just starting to figure that out when we bumped into each other that day in the coffee shop."

"What have you figured out since that day?"

"That I didn't have to die because Elizabeth did. And that's what I was doing, Zoey. Dying inside, little by little. Each day was worse than the one before, because I let that happen to me. But then I looked up and there you were." He squeezed her hand. "And I'm not going to tell you that the moment I set eyes on you I fell in love, or knew that we were meant to be or anything like that, because that's not what happened. Also, when I saw you that first time after Elizabeth's death, I certainly wasn't in a place where I could accept anything outside what I'd already known, so my feelings about that, about us, were… I don't know. Confused, maybe."

"Has that changed?" She asked the question, fearing the answer.

"Are you asking if I love you?"

Her hand still in his, Zoey scooted forward to the edge of her chair. "Do you?" she asked almost shyly.

"I fell in love with you at the fundraiser,

Zoey. And I've gone through hell dealing with it ever since, because I felt so guilty."

"Do you still feel guilty?"

"I put my wedding ring away today. And also Elizabeth's picture. It wasn't easy to do, but I had to, because what I've only just come to realize is that in loving you my guilt has disappeared. I can't totally put Elizabeth behind me because she was an important part of my life. And when you accept me, you have to accept that in me. The thing is…"

Daniel shut his eyes, withdrew his hand from Zoey's and ran his fingers through his hair. "The thing is…you're in my heart now." He opened his eyes slowly and looked across the table into Zoey's eyes. "In so many ways… ways that I probably don't even understand yet. Ways that I hope will continue to grow inside me. I want *us*, Zoey. You and me. In every way that a man can want a woman."

"But can you look at me and not compare me to Elizabeth? Because it scares me to death that you'll always cling to her as your standard."

"All I can say is trust me, and give me time to prove myself to you. I'll do it, Zoey. I'll do anything I have to, to gain your full trust. That is, if you love me. And maybe I should have asked you if you do before I started seeing the two of us well into the future."

"I do love you, Daniel. No qualms about that. And it wasn't love at first sight for me, either. But you did grow on me, starting with that night at the fundraiser."

"But it scares you," he stated.

"It scares me," she confirmed.

"What can I do to make it better? Because I'll do anything it takes."

This talk made her better. Understanding Daniel more made her better. The hope that was building inside her made her better. "Give me time. And, like you asked of me, be patient. Hold onto me when I try to push away—and I *will* try, Daniel. It's my nature. I retreat when I feel threatened." Nobody in her life had ever fought so hard for her, and it made her love Daniel all the more because he *was* fighting.

Daniel smiled. "Believe me, I'll hold on with everything I've got."

Zoey pushed back in her chair and stood up. She didn't move away from the table, though. Rather, she simply stood there for a moment and stared at Daniel, who had also risen from the table and was standing, staring back at her. "Are you sure I'm the one, Daniel? Because there hasn't been anybody else since Elizabeth, and I wonder if you should have looked around for a while. Maybe got yourself more used to being single again."

"I'm sorry I've put these doubts in you." Daniel walked around to Zoey's side of the table and pulled her into his arms. "That was never my intention."

"I put the doubts in me, Daniel. And Brad did. And even Elizabeth…" Nuzzling her head into his chest, she closed her eyes and a gentle sigh escaped her lips. This was where she wanted to be. The only place. But how could she stay there when so many doubts were still rattling around in her? "It's my problem to deal with."

"*Our* problem," he corrected. "Because you *are* the one. The only one. I don't need to play the field to see what else is out there because I found you, and you're all I want. And someday, Zoey, after I've reassured you every day that you're everything I need, I hope you trust me enough to believe me."

"I do trust you, Daniel. I trust what you tell me. But what I don't trust is that I'm enough for you. You've already had an ideal marriage and it worries me that I can't give you the same."

"But I don't want the same from you, Zoey. I don't expect it. What I want is everything that *you* are. I love you for who *you* are, for every-

thing *you* do, for the way *you* make me feel."
He pulled her even closer. "While I can't pretend to know what it feels like being the person who's stepping into my life, I can only hope that it's not too overwhelming, that you're not too weighed down by what I've had in my past. Because that was another time, another life. And I'm trying damned hard to move beyond that now. But I want to move beyond it with you. Only you."

She truly believed him. And that belief came with the love she felt for him. For Daniel, she wanted to be everything and, while her faith in herself was still wavering, he did instill a confidence in her like none she'd ever felt before. In time, and with Daniel's help, that confidence would grow. She was sure of it. "And I want to be there for you, Daniel, in every possible way. I want to be everything you need, because you're everything I need."

"Well, be warned. One of these days I'm going to ask you to marry me."

"You are?"

He lowered his head and he kissed her lightly on the forehead. "When you're ready,"

"How will you know when I'm ready?"

"Well, I could tell you it's something metaphysical, like the stars will all line up properly, or that I've had a vision of some sort. But I'd rather keep it a little more simple—stay close to you and watch over you for as long as it takes. Trust me, Zoey, I won't miss the clues."

"And Maddie?"

"She loves you already. I think she'll be excited to have you as her new mother."

"But I want her to remember Elizabeth," Zoey said. "I want her to know everything that Elizabeth was, and always make the distinction that Elizabeth was her mother. That's important."

"We'll do that for her. The two of us, together."

"I do love her. And I've got so many ideas of things she and I can do together..."

Before she finished her sentence, Daniel lowered his mouth to hers and she melted into his kiss like that was the place she had wanted to be for an eternity. "Want to continue this discussion in the bedroom?" she whispered into his ear once he had pulled slightly away from her.

Without a word, Daniel scooped her up into his arms and carried her down the hall. But he stopped at the bedroom door. "This is where it starts, Zoey," he said, his voice rough-edged.

Actually, it had started a year ago when he'd opened his front door to her and said, "Hello, I'm Daniel Caldwell." The road from that door to this one had taken more turns than she could ever have anticipated, but each and every turn had led her to the place she'd always wanted to be. With Daniel, for ever.

# EPILOGUE

He couldn't help but laugh at her. For all her athletic skills, Zoey was faking her bravery now, and it looked so cute on her. "The first thing you need to do is get yourself up to the edge of the hill."

Zoey clamped her ski poles into the snow and moved forward about an inch, then she stopped. "Do you know how far it is to the bottom?"

"Not as far as it was to the bottom of the hill I just skied." He pointed to the main hill on the course. It was a pretty straight slope, as far as ski slopes went, but it was also a fairly steep one.

"But you've been on skis before."

"And the next time I bring my girls out here, you'll have been on skis before, too."

Zoey looked down at Maddie, who'd already made her run down the beginner's hill, which the people at the ski lodge called "the bunny hill." She'd started more toward the bottom of the hill than the top, and had done a nice job of it, with only a couple falls in the few feet she'd skied. Right now, she was sitting in the snow, scooping it up and building a tiny castle. "Maddie did pretty good on her run, didn't she?"

"For a four-year-old, she was brilliant. And I think she really loved it."

"Because she takes after her father."

"And her father hopes to see her new mother do as brilliantly as her daughter did."

"That's putting a lot of pressure on me," Zoey grumbled.

"Just go to the edge and give yourself a shove."

"That's easy for you to say."

"You want me to shove you?" he teased.

"You shove me and that's the last thing you'll ever shove," she warned as she inched even closer to the edge.

"How about I take Maddie and we meet you down at the bottom?"

"You'd leave me here alone?"

"You're not going to back out, are you?"

She took a hard look down the hill and huffed out a frustrated breath. "Why does life with you have to be such an adventure?"

"Because you like it that way. Remember

those kayaks you bought a couple months ago? As I recall, that was *your* new adventure to explore."

"An adventure that didn't have me flying, uncontrolled, off the side of a mountain."

"They serve a nice oolong up at the lodge, if you'd rather do that while Maddie and I have another go at the bunny hill," he offered, knowing full well that his wife wouldn't hear of it.

She had a spirit like nothing he'd ever seen before, and there was no way Zoey would ever put herself in the position to be left behind. That was one of the things he loved most about her. Of course, the other things he loved… The list was long and growing every day. It was a full life, being married to Zoey, and he was happier than he'd imagined he ever could be.

"I hate oolong," she said through gritted teeth.

Daniel skied himself up next to Zoey and laid a reassuring hand across her back. "You can do this, you know."

Her full concentration was on the slope ahead of her now. "In due course," she said, beginning to take the proper stance, the way he'd taught her. But, once she'd assumed that stance, it was like she froze there. Didn't move. Didn't even blink. Barely even breathed. Finally, after a long pause, she said, "Do it, Daniel. Just do it."

"I thought you'd never ask," he said, smiling as he gave her that gentle nudge then watched her sail over the edge of the hill. She made it about halfway down before her left ski shot out from under her in one direction and her right in the other.

Daniel cringed, watching his wife's ungraceful descent. And, when it ended in the middle of the run, he reached for Maddie's hand. "I think we'd better go down to the bottom and collect your mother," he said. "And help her get back up here. Because, as stubborn as she is, she's going to want to keep trying this until she gets it right."

His wife, the perfectionist. It suited him. Zoey suited him. Life suited him again, thanks to Zoey. And that was everything he'd ever hoped for.

\* \* \* \* \*

*If you enjoyed this story,*
*check out these other great reads*
*from Dianne Drake:*


*DOCTOR, MUMMY...WIFE?*
*TORTURED BY HER TOUCH*
*A HOME FOR THE HOT-SHOT DOC*
*A DOCTOR'S CONFESSION*

*All available now!*